THE CITY OF SAND

THE CITY OF SAND

TIANXIA BACHANG

TRANSLATED FROM THE CHINESE
BY JEREMY TIANG

DELACORTE PRESS

Originally published in Chinese and in paperback by Anhui Arts Publishing
House, Hefei City, Anhui Province, China, in 2006.

Delacorte Press is a registered trademark and the colophon is a trademark of
Penguin Random House LLC.

Visit us on the Web! randomhouseteens.com

Educators and librarians, for a variety of teaching tools, visit us at
RHTeachersLibrarians.com

Library of Congress Cataloging-in-Publication Data
Names: Bachang, Tianxia.
Title: The city of sand / Tianxia Bachang.
Description: [New York] : Delacorte Press, [2017] | Summary: Teens Tianyi, his
best friend Kai, and Julie, a wealthy American, join with Professor Chen and
local guide Asat Amat to seek the lost city of Jinjue, hindered by lethal creatures
and an evil force.
Identifiers: LCCN 2017016508 (print) | LCCN 2017035182 (ebook) |
ISBN 978-0-553-52411-6 (ebook) | ISBN 978-0-553-52410-9 (hardback) |
ISBN 978-0-553-52413-0 (library binding)
Subjects: | CYAC: Adventure and adventurers—Fiction. | Buried treasure—
Fiction. | Supernatural—Fiction. | Deserts—Fiction. | Grave robbing—
Fiction. | Feng shui—Fiction. | China—Fiction.
Classification: LCC PZ.1.B265 (ebook) | LCC PZ.1.B265 Cit 2017 (print) |
DDC [Fic]—dc23

The text of this book is set in 13-point Perpetua.
Interior design by Ken Crossland

Printed in the United States of America
10 9 8 7 6 5 4 3 2 1
First American Edition

THE CITY OF SAND

PROLOGUE

Gold hunting is no picnic. It's not like going on vacation, and it's certainly not a dainty hobby like knitting or embroidery. If you're looking for something that dull, then you've come to the wrong person. What I practice is a craft, a technique of disruption. When the aristocratic families of ancient times built their graves, they were intent on keeping looters out, and they employed countless mechanisms to achieve that goal. You find all types of snares in these tombs: giant boulders rolling right at you, quicksand, poisoned arrows, venomous insects, and trapdoors set over spike-filled pits. You get the idea. During the Ming dynasty, when European technology reached China, newfangled Western equipment started putting in an appearance too, leading to some of the most intricate traps ever devised. In 1928, when the great warlord Sun Dianying wanted to break open the Eastern Tombs to use the treasures within to support his large army, it still took six days and a lot of explosives before he finally forced his way through. Can you imagine such a solid structure being built today? That's the mission of us gold hunters: breaking in with whatever means we have, dodging threats and lethal dangers until we get to the valuables buried alongside old-time nobility.

Of course, in this day and age, the bigger problem is actually finding those graves. All the ones with obvious earth mounds or stone markers have long since been dug up, so we have to search for tombs that lie deeper beneath the surface of the earth, the ones with no trace left aboveground. This requires a different set of skills, not to mention special tools, like Luoyang shovels—deep U-shaped shovels—bamboo nails, soil-eating dragons. That said, there are some experts who shun such tools, preferring to look for clues within ancient documents. A small number have more esoteric knowledge, such as the ability to read the veins and arteries of hills and rivers, and use the power of feng shui to locate these secret burial places. I belong to this select group. I've traveled to all sorts of places and experienced the most amazing things; if I were to list them one by one, your jaw would drop. You have no idea what mysteries lie in the ground beneath your feet, over seas and across rivers, past the earth and sky. I've forgotten what it means to be normal.

It all started with a book my grandfather left me—or rather, half a book.

CHAPTER ONE

MY GRANDFATHER GAVE ME MY NAME, TIANYI, WHICH MEANS "AS THE heavens intend." His name was Hu Guohua, and our family were once wealthy landowners, known for miles around. At their height, they had more than forty houses on three adjacent alleyways and could count important ministers and merchants among their number.

But as the saying goes, wealth never lasts past the third generation—no amount of money can buy restraint on the part of your descendants—and so by the time my grandfather was born, the Hu clan was poor once more. My grandfather didn't exactly help matters by getting addicted to opium as soon as he was of age. His small inheritance was quickly gone.

Never one to be deterred, my grandfather decided to

squeeze a bit of cash out of his uncle. Now, the uncle knew that Hu Guohua would only squander it away at the opium den, and refused to help him at first. He only changed his mind when my grandfather said he needed a loan to get married.

The old man was moved to tears that his nephew was finally going to make something of his life, with a virtuous woman to get him back on track. He handed over twenty silver dollars, saying how delighted he was that Guohua was giving up his vices, and adding that as soon as he had some time to spare, he'd come to visit his new niece.

You'd think this would stump my grandfather, but he was endlessly resourceful. As soon as he got home, he went to see the village paper craftsman, who made all the sacrificial goods to be burned for the dead. This artisan was extraordinarily skilled. Whatever you asked him to make—houses, carriages, livestock—he'd come up with detailed and realistic versions conjured from nothing but paper. It was easy for him to fulfill Guohua's request: a silhouette cut from white paper, features and clothes added with watercolor paint. He was done in no time, and as long as you didn't get too close, it looked just like a living person.

My grandfather brought his paper bride home and tucked her into bed. Taking a step back, he thought this should work—when his uncle came to visit, he'd just say his wife was too ill to receive visitors. The uncle wouldn't come past the front door, and from that distance the deception couldn't fail. Happy to have solved the problem so easily, he went out to get some opium, humming cheerfully.

A few weeks later, the uncle arrived with gifts for his

nephew's new wife. Guohua met him at the door and said how sorry he was that his wife was unwell, raising the curtain a little to give his uncle a peek at the woman tucked up in bed. Instead of being satisfied, however, his uncle got annoyed and said that that was no way to treat a relative. He wanted to greet the new wife in person, and if she was very sick, he was going to fetch a doctor.

My grandfather naturally came up with more excuses, but this just increased his uncle's suspicions. After they'd argued for a bit, the uncle pushed his way in and was confronted with a terrifying sight—a completely flat woman, face crudely smeared with rouge, blank eyes staring at the ceiling. When he realized what he was looking at, the uncle just about had a stroke. He died three days later—some said of anger.

Hu Guohua's entire family shunned him. They wouldn't even give him a spare grain of rice, never mind lending him money. Finally, he was reduced to selling a sandalwood chest that had belonged to his late mother for a couple of silver dollars. He'd wanted to keep it as a memento, but in the end his need for opium trumped that. Having exchanged the money for a small amount of the drug, he rushed back home to smoke it and soon was floating on blissful clouds.

He was abruptly brought down to earth when he noticed a dark shape crawling across his filthy bed. Bringing his eyes into focus, he saw a large mouse sitting not far from him. It was roughly the size of a cat. He knew it must be old because its whiskers were all white. It was sniffing away at the smoke coming from Guohua's nostrils, as if it knew what a good thing opium was and wanted to try some.

Amused, my grandfather said, "So you're an addict too? Come join in the fun." He took another deep drag from his pipe and blew a plume of smoke at the mouse. The creature didn't seem frightened. It lifted its nose to inhale deeply. After a short while, it seemed to have had enough and quickly scampered off.

For the next few days, the mouse showed up every day to sit by Guohua as he enjoyed his pipe. My grandfather was looked down on by everyone around him, despised by his family and neighbors. The mouse was the closest thing he had to a friend. Soon, if it was late showing up, he'd resist the urge to smoke until his companion had arrived.

Eventually, he ran out of things to sell, and his little hut contained only a bed and four walls. Sighing, my grandfather turned to his friend. "My dear mouse, this is the end of the road," he told the rodent. "No opium to share with you from now on." And with that, he burst into tears.

The mouse's eyes gleamed, as if it was thinking hard, and it turned to leave. At nightfall, it appeared, panting from the effort of dragging a silver coin to Guohua's bedside. My grandfather was overjoyed, and rushed straight into town to buy a hit of opium. Back home, he lit it from the lamp and lay back with the mouse, billows of contentment surrounding them.

The next day, the mouse brought in three more coins. Guohua didn't know how to thank it, so he did the only thing he could. "My friend mouse, you've stood by me in my hour of need, and you're my only true companion. Will you be my sworn brother?" From that time on, he called him Brother Mouse, sharing food and drink as well as opium, ripping up a sheet to make a little nest on the bed so the mouse could sleep there too.

They lived happily together. With the mouse bringing home at least a couple of coins a day, and sometimes as many as five, Guohua had nothing to worry about. In his later years, looking back, my grandfather would insist this time was the happiest of his life.

This bliss lasted six months, but as my grandfather's wealth quietly accumulated, he caught the attention of a villain: the village wastrel, Wang Ergang. Unlike the fallen Hu clan, the Wangs had never been wealthy, so Ergang rejoiced to see the Hus lose their fortune. It made him feel better to insult Guohua whenever he could—how did it feel to be down in the dirt with the rest of them?

And yet now it seemed Guohua was doing well. How could that be, when he appeared to have no source of income? Where was the money coming from, to fund all those opium fumes seeping from his house on a daily basis? Ergang decided to keep a close eye on Guohua. If it turned out he was stealing, Ergang would catch him in the act and drag him to the courthouse. There might even be a reward in it for him.

That didn't work. Apart from going into town now and then to buy food and opium, Guohua didn't seem to set foot outside the house. That just made Ergang itch to know what his source of income was. The next time Guohua went out for supplies, Ergang climbed over his wall and slipped into the house, ransacking the whole place in an effort to discover the secret. He found nothing, but then he saw an old mouse asleep on the bed. Thinking he could at least have some fun, he tossed the creature into a pot of water and slammed the lid on firmly, planning to hide nearby and have a good laugh when Guohua next went to get a drink.

Before he could conceal himself, though, my grandfather returned and immediately knew Ergang had harmed his only friend. He searched everywhere for Brother Mouse. When he finally lifted the lid of the water pot and saw his drowned friend, Guohua's eyes grew red, and he picked up a kitchen cleaver to attack Ergang. Fortunately, years of smoking opium had weakened his arms, and although Ergang was hit quite a few times, he escaped with his life, running bloodied to the nearest army outpost. The soldiers rushed to Guohua's house and arrested him.

When he was brought to the courthouse, the judge bellowed at him, demanding to know what had gotten into him, to attack another man in broad daylight.

Tears streaming down his face, my grandfather gave his account of the story from beginning to end. Still weeping, he concluded, "Back when I thought I had no way out, it was the mouse who helped me live. And now my sworn Brother Mouse is dead. If only I'd been at home to save him. I'll never have a friend like that again. Please punish me as you see fit for what I did to Wang Ergang. All I ask is that I be allowed to return home first to give my brother a good burial."

Before the judge could respond, the army captain was already sighing in sympathy. He said to Guohua, "Incredible. If that's how you feel about a mouse, how about a fellow human being? You seem like a good sort. Why not come be my deputy?"

In a time of war, might makes right, and a soldier's word

was law. The captain ordered his troops to beat Wang Ergang thoroughly and sent Guohua home to bury Brother Mouse. My grandfather carefully placed the mouse in a small wooden casket, wept over his body for half a day, then returned to throw in his fortune with the local army.

The Civil War was a time of great confusion, with a great many factions battling each other, and it was never clear who was on whose side. Alliances were constantly shifting; you might find yourself fighting alongside one group today, only to be at the other end of their gun barrels tomorrow. The troop my grandfather joined wasn't very large, and in less than a year, their territory had been taken over by another warlord. Those soldiers who survived fled in all directions, though sadly, the captain who'd taken my grandfather under his wing was killed by a single bullet.

His entire unit destroyed and disbanded, my grandfather could only go back home, where he found that his house had collapsed. He'd fled the battlefield virtually empty-handed and hadn't eaten for days. There was no alternative but to sell his handgun to local bandits, which bought a few days' food and a little plug of opium.

Now what? He had nowhere to turn, and his supplies would run out very soon. Then he remembered that just over a hundred miles away was a graveyard where many important officials lay. Surely their burial goods must be worth a fair bit.

The old Hu Guohua would have been too scared to desecrate a tomb, but this battle-hardened veteran had no such fears. He'd heard stories from his comrades about grave robbing—what they called reverse dipping—and how much money you could make from it. It was a capital crime, but what choice did he have? And so he made the arduous trek to the grave site, arriving on a near-moonless night, equipped with a sturdy shovel.

The sky was cloudless, but mist blocked most of the moonlight. Local folk said nights like this were when spirits liked to walk the earth. My grandfather drank the rice wine he'd brought with him for courage and peered out across the hillside. A cold wind whistled through the grass, and will-o'-the-wisps hovered over the graves. Now and then a strange bird cawed, like nothing he'd ever heard before. The lantern he'd brought guttered, as if it might go out at any minute.

At least there was no one in sight, so even if he cried out in fear, no one would hear. Guohua strode into the graveyard, singing folk songs for courage. Trembling, he found himself in the middle of the expanse, near a weed-strewn mound that, unlike all the tombs around it, didn't have a marker.

Even more strangely, the coffin wasn't buried, but stood wedged into the top of the mound. A portion of the box was exposed, and it looked new, painted a bright scarlet that glistened in the faint light.

Doubts niggled at my grandfather. What was this doing here? Was it some sort of trick? But he was here now, and there was a grave he wouldn't even have to dig into to rob, so why not start with this one? He was going to die anyway, either from starvation or opium withdrawal; it might be easier to get killed by an angry ghost. He'd suffered enough for one lifetime—what did he have to lose?

Having reached a decision, he raised his shovel high, then dug it into the soil, clearing a space around the coffin so he could see the whole thing. It took a long time—years of opium addiction had also weakened his lungs, and he had to keep stopping to catch his breath. When he was finally done, he was not in a hurry to get the lid off. He slumped against the coffin for a rest, digging in his pockets for an opium hit.

A few puffs on his pipe settled his nerves and gave him strength, and with a grunt he pulled himself to his feet, cracking open the lid with his shovel. The corpse within was a beautiful woman, looking like she'd just fallen asleep. There was thick makeup on her face. Smears of rouge across her cheeks blazed beneath the white powder that covered every inch of exposed skin. Her body was draped in bright red satin robes: a bridal dress.

Had she just been buried? This graveyard had been abandoned long ago, so where had she come from? But if this was an older grave, then surely she would have decomposed?

Although these questions troubled my grandfather, he was past caring. His attention was mostly occupied by the jewelry she was wearing. There were all kinds of gems, glittering in the light from his lantern, not to mention the mounds of silver dollars wrapped in red packets, gold bars next to them. So much wealth he could barely count it.

He was rich now. All he had to do was reach in and help himself. The emerald ring on the woman's finger was most enticing. He made to grab it when a hand closed around his wrist.

Had the corpse come to life? No, she lay undisturbed. Filled with terror, my grandfather turned to see a tall man glaring at him.

The man was named Sun, a renowned feng shui master. My grandfather had passed him on the road, and Master Sun had sensed a dark energy coming off him. He explained all this later—how he'd known immediately that Guohua was up to no good and had guessed that he must be heading to this burial site to despoil it. So he'd turned around and kept an eye on him.

Master Sun clutched my grandfather's wrist, snarling, "Thief! I have only one question for you: aren't you afraid of heaven's retribution?"

Scared out of his wits, my grandfather knelt and begged for Master Sun's forgiveness.

The older man raised him to his feet. "You might be walking down a bad path," he said, "but you've done no great wrong yet. It's not too late to mend your ways. I can help, if you like, but you'll have to become my disciple. And you'll need to give up your opium pipe."

Guohua thought for a while. Giving up opium seemed impossible, but he might as well agree for now. So he knelt and kowtowed to Master Sun eight times for luck.

Master Sun urged his new disciple to help him put the lid back on the coffin. It wasn't natural that this woman's corpse was so well-preserved. Could it be that this graveyard was a breeding ground for the undead? They quickly nailed the coffin tightly shut, then marked crisscrossing lines in black ink over its entire surface. The lines would act as a giant black net, preventing what was inside from breaking free.

Next, Master Sun told my grandfather to gather some dried branches. When they had enough kindling, they set the brightly painted coffin on fire. It burned with such black, evil-smelling smoke, they knew it must have contained something foul. My grandfather lingered, hoping to pick the valuables out of the ashes, but Master Sun didn't take his eyes off him, and finally he had to give up and follow his new boss home.

The first thing Master Sun did was mix some secret herbs to rid my grandfather of his addiction. Over the next few weeks, he taught Guohua the basics of feng shui divination, until Guohua was able to run a stall in the nearby city, telling fortunes for a small fee. He married a local girl and, grateful to Master Sun for setting his life back in order, never misbehaved again.

After some years, Master Sun got pneumonia and never recovered. On his deathbed, he beckoned my grandfather to lean close and said, "You've been my loyal disciple all this while, and I still haven't managed to teach you everything I know. But here. I have an ancient book: *The Sixteen Mysteries of Yin-Yang Feng Shui*. There's only half of it left—someone ripped away the final chapters before I got to it—but there's plenty of knowledge in it, grave-craft and all sorts of useful things. Keep it in remembrance of me." And with that, he let out a last breath and expired.

Hu Guohua buried his master and devoted the rest of his life to studying that book. He learned a lot of secrets and was able to make a good living telling wealthy folk from the city where the best places were to situate their family graves, what days were most suited for wedding banquets, and other such auspicious tips. He also had a son—Hu Yunxuan, my father. Although a fervent rebel in his student days, Yunxuan eventually settled down into a plodding existence as a low-level policeman, married my mother, and had me.

My grandfather isn't with us anymore. Just before he died,

he secretly slipped that old feng shui book to me, saying not to let my father know. My father didn't approve of my dabbling in the supernatural. I studied the book in secret and became an expert on its teachings by the time I was a teenager. I knew that this knowledge had mostly vanished from the world, and that my grandfather had left me a rare gift. *The Sixteen Mysteries of Yin-Yang Feng Shui,* I was sure, would help me break out of my dull, small-town life and put me on the path toward adventure.

CHAPTER TWO

THE SUMMER I TURNED SEVENTEEN, I WENT WITH MY BEST FRIEND, Wang Kaixuan, in search of the catacombs of Wild Man Valley. There was no guarantee they were actually there, but now and then antiques would show up in the river that runs through our village, and someone would say, "These didn't sprout from the water. They must have washed down from the hills." The story was that Liao nobles and their fortunes were buried up there, but so many ghost stories surrounded the area that no one dared go in search of the treasure.

We were scared too, of course, but I believed the knowledge I'd gained from my grandfather would keep us safe. Having studied his book thoroughly, I was determined to be one of the good ones—a gold hunter. People these days confuse gold hunting with grave robbing, but everything in the world has two sides, so good things can turn bad and bad things can turn to good. Gold hunting is the good side.

Look at it this way: upper-class graves are full of valuable objects. Can those things really be said to belong to the resident of each tomb? Isn't it more likely that these aristocrats looted them from the people, and we're simply taking back what belongs to us? After all, there's no point in leaving these things to molder in the ground, next to a pile of dry bones sunk into eternal sleep.

During the long trek over the hills into Wild Man Valley, I told Kai what we might expect. He was my oldest friend, but we'd never really talked about gold hunting before. My father didn't like the subject, insisting I should study hard and go to a good university instead of fooling around with what he called "this nonsense." But I felt I was ready to turn my secret knowledge into action.

Truth be told, Kaixuan didn't seem to be paying much attention to me. We were on a steep path, and he was breathing hard, his round face alarmingly red. His friends called him Kai. Both of us had on large rucksacks containing everything we'd need for our expedition, but his seemed in danger of actually dragging him backward.

"Have you been listening to a word I've said?"

"Of course," Kai grunted, struggling to get the words through his throat. "You said the Hu family has been doing this for generations, and you, Hu Tianyi, are not a grave robber."

"What's the difference?" I quizzed him.

He grimaced and shook his head. "I forget."

"'Gold hunting is a gentlemanly pursuit, and should only

be undertaken with care,'" I lectured, quoting my grand-father's words from memory. "'Amateurs might gouge great scars into the earth, scrabbling for pennies and leaving only carnage behind. We hold ourselves to a higher standard, open-ing tombs of the highest quality, and only with the consent of the deceased.'"

Despite his agony, Kai burst out laughing. "That's a good one! I'll be sure to ask each corpse for permission."

I swatted his arm. "You really weren't paying attention. Didn't you hear me say we have to light a candle in each room?"

"Sure. Otherwise how would we see what we're doing?"

"No, idiot. We have flashlights for that. The candles—"

"Then why am I carrying this rucksack full of them?"

"I'm telling you. And I've got the water and ropes, which are heavier. Listen, you have to place a candle in the south-eastern corner of the burial chamber. Then you help yourself to the jewels—they'll be stuffed in mouths and hands, or placed over the chest—but very gently, and always being sure to leave one or two behind. If there's any objection from the deceased, the candle goes out. If that happens, you replace everything, kowtow three times, and run as quickly as you can."

"These people died like a thousand years ago. Why wouldn't their spirits be reincarnated like everyone else's?" Kai asked. "Why hang around in a dingy, musty tomb?"

"Who knows? Maybe these are the ones that couldn't give up their worldly possessions."

We squabbled as we continued our way to the top of the hill. We'd set off early that morning, telling our parents we were going on a hike. There has to be some advantage to living in the middle of nowhere—a tiny village in the Liaoning hills, hundreds of miles from the nearest city—and for us, it was that the Liao tombs were within walking distance. We might even be the first gold hunters to discover them—maybe then my dad would have to start taking me seriously. I was confident that as long as we located the cave, I'd be able to sniff out what lay hidden in it. Part of my knowledge came from my grandfather's book, but most came from listening to his stories when I was little.

Our feet crunched over layers of dry leaves, surrounded on all sides by tall, thin trees—pine, birch, and poplar, growing so close hardly any light filtered through. I began using a stick to probe the ground—there was always the danger that leaves were concealing a hole or a marshy patch that might swallow us up. All around was a faint scent of decay.

At the top of the ridge, overlooking Wild Man Valley, the trees began to thin out, leaving only scrubby grass and bushes, primeval forest ceding ground to Mongolian plains. Suddenly, we could see the wide sky and the huge red orb dipping below the far hills. The whole vista was full of puffy crimson clouds, dense as an oil painting, as if the sun were bleeding.

"What a sight," Kai said, mopping his brow. "At least we haven't come here for nothing."

I pulled out my compass and quickly did an eight-symbol reading, using the octagonal *bagua* to map out the valley's shape. Everything was right, as predicted in *The Sixteen Mysteries of Yin-Yang Feng Shui*—there were definitely noble tombs. Now all we had to do was wait—the book said when the moon reached its zenith, it would shine directly onto their location.

Flopping down next to our rucksacks, we watched the color leach from the sky, moving again only when it was completely dark. I kept one eye on the moon and the other on my compass, and it wasn't long before I'd pinpointed the cave. Of course, these hills were dotted with all kinds of burial sites, but if we wanted the most important one, it was just beneath our feet. We pulled our shovels from our rucksacks and began digging.

As the earth piled up around us, Kai grew anxious. "Tianyi, what if we see a ghost?"

"That's just superstition," I reassured him.

"But the candles?"

"Here's the scientific explanation: the candles are to make sure the air is good. You know how poisonous gases can build up underground? If the flame goes out, there's definitely not enough oxygen, and we know to get out as soon as we can."

His fears allayed, Kai dug in with gusto, no doubt motivated by thoughts of coffins stuffed with jewels. As for me, I was nervous too—my grandfather had definitely alluded to seeing what he called unclean beings—but we'd deal with anything of that nature when we came to it.

Soon we had a hole about the size of a bucket, wide enough for a skinny body like mine, though a tight fit for Kai, who was bigger than I was. Our shovels began hitting empty air. I shined my flashlight into the blackness reaching far down below. I could just make out the walls, which didn't look like they'd been carved out by human hands—more by some giant beast with extremely sharp claws.

Nothing for it but to jump in. There was some danger, of course—tombs of this era had sophisticated security, not like crude Tang dynasty safeguards with their falling rocks and trip wires. These Liao graves were more likely to have jars of dragon oil that roared to life when exposed to air and engulfed intruders in flame. I hoped my gold-hunter's knowledge would allow me to spot anything like that.

Kai landed with a thump beside me, the soft earth providing a gentle landing. I already had my flashlight out, and was examining the small chamber we found ourselves in. It was mostly empty, except for some animal skins hung on the walls and three lumps in one corner. I had to stifle a cry when I realized the lumps were dead bodies, so far gone their skin was black and clinging to their bones, ants crawling in and out of their eye sockets.

Kai's jaw dropped. "Tianyi. Are these the wild men?"

I shook my head. "Whoever heard of a savage wearing clothes?"

The coats that wrapped the bodies could only be a few decades old. I plucked a metallic button off a collar and examined it. A military emblem, but not all the symbols were familiar. Then, in a flash, I realized who they were—and also where the stories about wild men in the valley had come from. These were Japanese soldiers.

I told Kai, who seemed bewildered. "But why?" he muttered. "Why would they be here? I thought the devils went home after they surrendered."

My history was a bit hazy, but I did remember what else happened in 1945, just before the Japanese surrendered: the Soviets bombed the invading Japanese forces in Northeast China, and the surviving soldiers scattered into the forests. These soldiers must have stumbled onto this cave and hidden out, maybe growing old here, certainly dying. While they were alive, their clothes must have grown tattered and their beards long, so any villagers sighting them would have thought these were wild men of the woods.

One mystery solved, and it was barely past midnight! Not bad, but there'd be nothing here for us. We'd need to head farther in. First we reached into our rucksacks for our masks, which hung neatly from our ears, covering our mouth and nose completely. It's unseemly to leave living breath inside a grave, or even worse, to accidentally breathe life into a corpse.

A low tunnel led to more rooms, though there was no sign that the Japanese soldiers had made it this far. We pressed on through these bubbles of air in the soft, dark earth, some empty, some holding less-important tombs—concubines or servants, buried with their lord.

Finally, we came to the main burial chamber, at least a hundred feet square, with a courtyard before it, as if this were a regular home. There was no platform for the tomb, only a shallow indentation with the coffin sunk into it: a tomb within a tomb. The walls were tiled and painted over with a series of scenes, the colors as vivid as the day they were created. Some showed hunting scenes, others some kind of banquet. All of them featured a man in a fox-fur coat. This must be the lord whose grave we were visiting.

We quickly explored the surrounding rooms, marveling at the riches within. There were anterooms to the left and right, each crammed with porcelain urns and other ceramics. To the rear were the skeletons of four horses—buried with the man whose chariot they'd pulled—and a few suits of armor. Finally, we got down to business. I lit a candle in the southeast corner of the room, pulling out my compass for verification, then knelt before the sunken coffin.

It was a sizable box of rosewood inlaid with gold decorations. I touched it reverently. The wood was heavier than what regular people could have afforded, made from the very core of a tree. Carefully, I pushed a chisel into the line where the lid fit on, and Kai did the same on the other side. With a creak, the smallest gap appeared. We did the same all down the sides, prying nail after nail loose, little explosions of dust making us cough through our masks.

As the last nail popped up, I grinned. "What do you think we'll find inside?"

"Something worth a whole bunch of yuan, I hope!" Kai said.

I deepened my voice. "You know, there's a prophecy about two grave robbers, one fat and one skinny. They venture into a deep, dark burial chamber and see a coffin that opens the tiniest crack, and a huge arm shoots out, covered in green fur, with fingernails three inches long—"

Kai let out a little shriek. "Stop it!"

"It grabs the fat one and pulls him into the coffin, and there's nothing left of him but his final, bloodcurdling scream. The other guy runs away in time."

"No more messing around! You almost scared me to death."

We took hold of the wooden lid and heaved it to the floor with a crash, after which the silence seemed deeper than before. Inside the coffin lay a tall man, all the moisture in his body shriveled away, leaving bruised-looking purple skin hugging bones. This corpse had to be a thousand years old—there were nothing but black holes where the eyes and nose should have been. The man wore a faded scarlet robe with tattered gold embroidery and a wrinkled, mold-spotted pair of cloud-striding boots.

My scalp prickled, but excitement was stronger than fear. Clasping my hands, I recited the ancient prayer: "Revered sir, we are poor and have no choice but to take a few small articles from you. No offense is intended, for you have long departed into the sky and into the ground, dust to dust, earth to earth. Your wealth is only external—you didn't bring it with you into this world, nor can you take it with you. These treasures will improve the lives of many like us—"

Before I could finish, Kai was already reaching into the coffin, feeling around for anything valuable. He took out a tricolor water jar. "Careful!" I hissed. "Don't disturb the body." He continued rooting away, and I picked up one of the urns next to us, the better to hold any jewels we might find. Despite myself, I was trembling. I was a gold hunter now!

My own hand landed on something cool and hard. Jade—even better. Gold fetched a high price, but jade was priceless. This piece was exquisitely carved into a pair of wings—a moth. Song dynasty, by the look of it. How much would this be worth? I stood still, admiring it, thinking how many yuan it would fetch from a Hong Kong or Taiwan buyer. Tens of thousands, at least. Was there even such a thing as a ten-thousand-yuan note? Lost in my fantasies, it took me a second to realize Kai had gasped loudly and was now staring in alarm at something behind me.

Turning around, I saw nothing at first. Then I realized: sometime in the last few minutes, our candle had gone out.

CHAPTER THREE

FROM THE SWEAT BEADING EVERY INCH OF HIS FACE, I COULD TELL KAI was as terrified as I was. Why hadn't I planned better for this eventuality? My grandfather had always stressed the importance of the candle, but I don't think he'd ever had a ghost blow it out on him.

Moving quickly, we hauled the lid back into place, then stood facing each other. Nothing stirred. "Tianyi," whispered Kai. "How much did you pay for that candle?"

I shrugged. It was from the village shop. "Probably two cents?"

"Maybe you should have sprung for a five-cent one."

"Fine, next time I'll invest in a fancy candle. Imported

from America, if you like. But this one's gone out now. Let's put things back as quickly as we can."

Still neither of us moved. It had cost us so much effort to come here, not to mention the trouble we'd get into when we got back home. All that, just to leave empty-handed? I walked over to the corner and lit the candle again. "How about if we put a couple of things back and see if it goes out this time."

Bargaining with a corpse in this way was definitely not in the gold-hunting manual, but that first extinguishing could have been the wind. Kai placed the water jar on the lid of the coffin, too lazy to open it again. I turned to smile at him, but he was pointing a trembling finger at the corner. "Tianyi, the flame. Why is the flame . . . green?"

Sure enough, the candle was glowing a brilliant emerald-green, tinting the whole room an eerie shade. As we watched slack-jawed, it flickered twice, then winked out with a defiant pop.

This wasn't good. Grabbing Kai's arm, I ran for the exit. Staying a minute longer would probably mean staying forever, becoming part of the Liao kingdom's grave goods. A rush of air came toward us, and instinct told me to duck, just in time to avoid the tricolor jar, which flew over my head and splintered against the far wall. Following it was the coffin lid, which wedged itself neatly into our exit. Great.

Kai's howl was terrifying. "Tianyi, talk to him," he pleaded. "We can leave more stuff behind, we can leave it all. It's not good to make him angry."

Too late for that, I knew. I watched as the corpse clambered out of his box. Alarmingly, a layer of thick red fur had sprouted across his body. My breath grew cold inside me. I hadn't been entirely joking about the green-haired corpse—my grandfather had said that could happen in a body dead from poison. But what did red hair mean?

This was definitely not the time for questions. I grabbed my black donkey hoof from my rucksack and flung it. The hoof was meant to be a powerful charm, but the corpse easily swatted it aside, then reached for our shovels, which it hurled against the ceiling. Only inches away from the corpse, we swerved and made for the only feasible exit—the rear room. In his haste, Kai kicked over a tall urn. The red-haired demon apparently couldn't see, and stumbled over it, emitting a sobbing cry like the call of a wild cat.

I swiveled and, ducking under the corpse's arm, stood directly behind it. This was no ghost, but a being of solid flesh, smelling absolutely fetid. Wrapping one arm around its neck, I clung on. Its limbs were too death-stiffened for it to reach backward. This was the safest place to be.

Just as I was wondering how long I'd be able to stay in this position, a light dazzled me. It was Kai, sprinting over with his flashlight in one hand and, in the other, a wolf-tooth lance he'd liberated from one of the suits of armor. It must have weighed at least twenty pounds, and he was holding it with difficulty. When I judged the moment right, I let go of the corpse and jumped aside, and the lance struck home. Like all the metal here, it was rusty and aged, but this wasn't a weapon that relied on a sharp edge—simple brute force was all it took, and with the full bulk of Kai behind it, the wolf tooth impaled the red-haired corpse and pinned it to the ground.

For at least a minute, we simply stood where we were,

breathing in great gulps of musty air, our heartbeats seeming to echo through the room. We'd used every ounce of energy in our bodies and needed to recharge.

"Kai," I said uncertainly, "he's still twitching. Should we hit him again?"

"Yes, over the head this time."

Barely were the words spoken before the red-haired creature bounced up as if on springs, propelling the lance back into the rear room. I swore at our horrible luck. We needed that lance. Now that our shovels were lodged in the ceiling, it was the only tool we had to break through the coffin lid blocking our exit.

Right now, though, the big problem was that the reanimated corpse was shambling toward us. We dashed into the back chamber, where we found that the lance had bashed a hole through the far wall. A hole? Was there a secret room beyond this one? I shined my flashlight through, but it hit nothing, just emptiness. A tunnel, not a room.

A blast of cold air announced the arrival of our red-haired friend. No time to think—I bashed the lance at the hole, widening it enough that we could wriggle through. The corpse didn't seem able to come any farther. It was walking again and again into the wall.

Suddenly, I noticed something. "Kai! Your gloves—why aren't you wearing them?"

"I got all sweaty opening the coffin, so I took them off."

"Are you crazy? Touching a corpse with living hands—that's what brought it back!"

"Don't blame me. It's a dead body, not a land mine."

We were interrupted by a crash as the wall splintered a

little more under the creature's assault. Time to go. We crawled along as quickly as possible. Soon the tunnel widened, and the floor became concrete. As soon as we could stand, we started running, imagining we could smell the corpse's wretched stench right behind us.

The passage ended in a sort of bunker, which mercifully had a huge metal door. As soon as we were in, Kai and I leaned hard against it till the hinges, rusty from decades of disuse, began to move. Any moment now, I expected a red-haired arm to reach through the opening, but with a final shudder, the massive door closed. We were in another part of the underground complex, presumably built by the Japanese as an air-raid shelter. Unless the corpse had more strength than an American warhead, he wouldn't be breaking through anytime soon.

My fears allayed for the moment, I waited for my breath to steady, then shined my flashlight around, trying to get a sense of where we were. The bunker was massive, piled high with all kinds of supplies. The Japanese had built places like this all over Manchuria, to maintain the front against the Soviets.

"Tianyi?" Kai's voice broke into my thoughts. "That thing—do you know what it is?"

I hadn't really had time to consider the red-haired corpse, but now I ran my grandfather's stories through my head. "It's a revenant," I said. "The ancient Manchurians had a trick of writing out a curse and burning the paper, then sprinkling the ashes into the deceased's mouth before burial. It reanimates the body when anyone tries to steal from the dead. It's relentless—the corpse won't rest again until . . ."

"Until what?"

I swallowed hard. "Until the thieves are dead."

There was a momentary silence. "Well," Kai said stoutly, "I don't think we count as thieves. Did we even get any loot?"

As a matter of fact, we'd managed to drop most of our bounty while fleeing. Digging through my pockets, I could only find the jade moth. But . . .

"What's going on?" Kai gasped as I pulled it out.

I couldn't explain it either—the vivid green of the wings was now a dull yellow. "Maybe it's the light?" I muttered, realizing just how little I knew. Reading half an ancient manual hadn't made me an expert at all.

The fortress was laid out like a maze. To keep from getting too lost, we felt our way along the outer wall, looking for an exit. Shining the flashlight up, I could see clusters of emergency lights and wires. If only we could find some way to turn the electricity on! Groping our way along, we found our path narrowing to a passage that sloped upward into stairs. I led the way up, and just as I reached the top, Kai stumbled with a muffled curse, pitching us both forward.

We landed in a huge stone cave, every surface covered in glossy green moss and a slick of damp. Countless bulky shapes hung overhead. We strained to see through the gloom, and it took us a good few seconds to work out what those shapes were. When we did, we almost screamed in terror. They were giant bats, far bigger than any others I'd encountered, clinging to the walls with their wings wrapped tightly around themselves.

As we gaped, those wings began to unfurl. Our clattering entrance had shaken them from their dreams and they were rousing, yawning to reveal mouths full of long fangs. The bats had round faces and pointy ears and cruelly sharp spikes at each joint of their wings. They'd been using this underground lair as a home and were now prepared to defend it.

When the first few swooped toward us, I grabbed the closest thing to hand—a stick I spotted in a nearby pile of debris—and lashed out. They retreated a few feet, close enough to swipe with their razorlike claws, drawing blood. My feet slipped on a floor that I could now see was covered in guano and the carcasses of small animals. There was no way we could fight off such numbers, so before the main assault began, I reached into my rucksack for the flare gun I'd brought just in case. I'd had to save up to get it mail-order, but it was worth every cent now. When I fired into the heaving black mass circling us, the flaming charge rocketed toward the roof, sparks cascading off it, and the bats shrieked in terror at the sudden heat and blazing light, rising in a flock to the ceiling vent, chattering in their high-pitched language of squeaks. There must have been a thousand of them.

The light grew so intense I covered my face with my arms, remaining still until the flapping noises stopped. Groping for my flashlight, I called out to Kai and he grunted weakly in response, apparently scared out of his wits. When I found the light, its faint beam barely registered, but as my eyes adjusted, I could see that the bats were completely gone. Just as well; I didn't have a backup flare for the gun.

A thump came from behind me. I swung around, but the bat that had just landed was motionless, its wings twisted. A hole in its chest still smoldered; it had been hit by the flare. There was no further movement.

What next? There was still no way out. The vent the bats had left through was far higher than we could reach, and the revenant would still be guarding the outer metal door. As I was chewing over our options, Kai slumped to the floor, groaning, "Do we have any food left? I'm so hungry I can't think."

I could have done with something to eat too, but the fruit and buns we'd brought were long gone. Then it occurred to me there was a giant dead bat in the cave with us. Well, why not? We eat field mice and grasshoppers; this couldn't be much different.

Kai thought it was worth a try too. I sent him back to the bunker for some wooden crates to burn—we could have used the coffins as fuel, but I didn't want to anger any more spirits—while I got on with skinning the bat and tying it to the stick as a makeshift spit. When Kai returned, I stamped the crates into boards, then whittled one with my knife to produce shavings for kindling. Before long, the beast was hanging over a crackling fire, and Kai was sniffing appreciatively. "Smells like mutton," he said.

As soon as the meat was ready, we began hacking bits off and gnawing enthusiastically. A couple of water droplets landed on my head, but I was too busy chewing to pay much attention. Kai flinched, apparently feeling the same thing. "That's funny. I didn't notice it raining." As the words left his mouth, we both realized something was wrong and slowly raised our heads.

CHAPTER FOUR

ABOVE US, JUST WHERE THE FIRELIGHT MET DARKNESS, SOMETHING was watching, something with a face twice as big as a human's: bloodshot eyes above a hooked nose, protuberant lips bracketing a great cavern of a mouth. As we watched, a blood-red tongue emerged from it, dripping drool. The smell of roasting meat had summoned it.

What kind of creature was this? The skin on its neck was black and coarse, and as it leaped from its perch near the roof, we could see its whole body—like a bear's, but more agile. I tore off a chunk of meat and flung it as far from us as possible, and the beast sprang for it, its spine curved like a bow. I'd seen pictures of this animal before—what was the name? Ah yes, the great sloth. Normally as slow-moving as its name implied, this one seemed to have been galvanized by the savory aroma of our meal.

Kai flung more meat in its direction, but it ignored that and kept ambling toward us. Turning to me, his lips dry, Kai said, "I think he might . . . think we're bats."

Unwilling to be a sloth's dinner, we turned to run. I'd barely gone two steps before I stumbled over something, almost smashing my knee. Kai crashed into me as I went down, delaying us both long enough for the sloth to catch up. It lunged at Kai first, no doubt sensing there was more flesh on him. The knife we'd been using to hack off bits of roast meat was just within reach. I grabbed it and turned to plunge it to the hilt in the beast's front limb. Red-hot after being by the fire so long, the blade seared the creature's flesh as it went in, stunning it into retreating a few paces, steam rising from its wound.

Looking up, we saw that more sloths had appeared while we were distracted, and were rapidly descending the cavern walls. Fortunately, they seemed to be afraid of the fire, and as long as we huddled close enough to the flames, we were safe for the time being.

Pulling a blazing plank from the heap, I thrust it at the smallest sloth, singeing its skin, and it shrank away, curling up protectively. We backed off slowly, each clutching a flaming piece of wood in one hand. The sloths followed but kept their distance. We retraced our steps all the way through the bunker, not daring to try any of the other passages in case they were dead ends, ending up against the metal door.

My initial idea had been to think of an alternative escape route once we were fortified with bat meat, but the sloth assault had come too suddenly for that. Our torches were burning lower and would soon be blackened stumps, leaving us defenseless.

There was nowhere else we could retreat. While Kai flung our torches toward the beasts, causing them to dart backward, I dragged the door open, bracing myself, but the revenant was nowhere to be seen. Kai scooted through and we pushed it shut, leaning against it with all our might, not sure we'd be strong enough to hold it against a sloth's massive weight.

A gust of icy wind came around the corner, and then the red-haired corpse itself. It had just been patrolling the corridor, and now it leaped, forcing me to duck. Suddenly released, the door flew open, knocking Kai aside as the largest sloth of the pack bounded in. It entered with such force that the revenant was knocked to the ground, but it bounced back up immediately, reaching its arms out to impale the sloth on the ends of its fingernails, which were the size and sharpness of steel knives.

The sloth's yelps of pain brought the rest of its clan scurrying. The smallest quickly had its head lopped off by those unnatural nails. Then two of them latched on to the corpse's arms, which were unable to bend, and managed to snap one. Kai and I backed away, feeling unspeakably lucky. We had been pursued by two enemies, only to have them attack each other instead!

Moving as fast as we could, we crept back into the room with the tombs. We were back where we'd started, with nothing to show for it. Not only had we acquired no treasure, we'd attracted the ire of a reanimated corpse and some oversized mammals. This had not been a successful gold-hunting expedition. At least I was able to snatch my black donkey hoof from the ground.

The coffin lid still blocked our exit, but a few blows from the lance broke a hole in it. Kai went first, but before I could follow, there was a roar like thunder and two giant sloths lurched into the room, streaked with blood and seemingly in a frenzy from their wounds. Their red eyes flashed with rage when they saw me.

With Kai urging me to hurry from the other side of the wall, I picked up a small rock and flung it at the crystal-glazed tiles above the main coffin. As I'd expected, they'd been booby-trapped, and dragon oil poured down into the room, igniting as soon as it hit the air and engulfing the sloths. Leaving them writhing as great spouts of flame destroyed everything behind us, I made my exit.

The last steps seemed to take no time at all, and we were staring up at the night sky. Again, Kai went first, lowering a rope behind him for me to climb out. Just like that, we were free. It felt amazing being in the open air again, back in the regular world. As we walked away, the sun was just starting to peek over the eastern ridge, the color of spilled blood.

I thought of how I'd never truly believed in ghosts, despite my grandfather's stories. Now I understood how foolish that was, like a hunter who'd gone into a forest and, not spotting any prey, declared there were no wild animals. In this world, we only experience a tiny amount of what is possible. What can we do for the vast number of things we will never know about except treat them with respect?

Neither of us had the energy to talk much. In any case,

we had other problems—first the long trek down the hill on wobbly legs, and then facing our parents. It wasn't too bad for Kai, who only had his mother to deal with, but when I stumbled into our courtyard around noon, clothes tattered, scorched, and covered in guano, face smeared with red earth, my father was so furious he could barely speak.

After I'd gotten cleaned up and had something to eat, my father tried to stay calm as he said they'd been worried sick when I didn't come home all night. When I told him where I'd been, he exploded again.

"Wild Man Valley! Everyone knows that's the most dangerous place around here—you could have been eaten by all kinds of creatures! Haven't you heard those stories of people stepping on a pile of leaves, only to get sucked into the quicksand hiding underneath? Then there are the wild men—heaven protect you if you encounter one of those."

"I know, Dad." Truth be told, it was my mother's quiet sobbing that hurt me more.

"Yes, you know. You know everything. I blame your grandfather for putting ideas in your head. Telling you all kinds of stories."

"It's not Grandpa's fault. I'm old enough to know my own mind."

"Right, you're grown up now. Your wings are fledged and you're ready to fly. Fine, go ahead, but I'm warning you—if you continue with these shenanigans, you can forget about coming back to this house again."

His words were still echoing in my ears when I met Kai later that day. We were both determined to go on—me because I thought it was what my grandfather would have wanted, him because he had dreams of getting rich quick. Besides, neither of us had much else to look forward to. Even if we worked hard at school, it would be a miracle to get into university, not to mention getting any kind of decent job.

Buying the train tickets to Beijing took out a huge chunk of our savings, but there was no option. Our small town was no place to pursue gold hunting. With a small bag packed, the jade piece safely tucked away in one pocket, and the rest of my cash in a bundle, I said goodbye to my weeping mother and promised to stay safe. My father kept his back turned, and I left with a heavy heart, hoping he would change his mind when I returned successful.

The train chugged through the night toward the capital city, and I could barely sleep for thinking what awaited us there. I'd never gone outside my home province before, so I relied on half-remembered tales of my grandfather's wanderings for guidance. The next morning, we asked directions, and a short bus ride later, we had found our way to Pan Market, the place to go for antiques. All we found was an assortment of old vases, decrepit watches and clocks, three-inch-long embroidered shoes for bound feet, valueless bronze money, snuffboxes—objects most people had lying around the house. Still, in the midst of this plenty, my discolored little jade moth seemed too insignificant to bring out.

Kai, though, had something special: a jade amulet he always carried with him. He'd inherited it from his father, who'd liberated it from a bandit's body during his time in the army in Xinjiang. The jade piece was oddly shaped and ancient-looking, covered with pictographs that might have been a map or some archaic language.

I'd seen that amulet many times. Kai had shown it to me because I knew a lot about antiques through my grandfather's stories. On this one, though, I drew a blank—nothing like it was mentioned in the manual.

Seeing the antiques stalls, Kai was ready to offer up his jade for appraisal, but I grabbed his arm. "This is the only thing you have to remember your father by. Don't part with it so quickly—we're not desperate yet."

Casually lingering by stall after stall, fingering the merchandise, we came to one where the goods seemed a notch above the garbage everyone else had. The old guy running the place had a weathered face. A single gold tooth gleamed incongruously in his mouth. We got to chatting, and he told us he was from Hainan Island. His dad had been a craft finder, so he had enough old artifacts with him to start a small antiques stall.

"Craft finder"—wasn't that just a fancy way of saying he'd gotten the stuff out of tombs? Other people might not have noticed, but I hadn't been brought up on my grandfather's stories for nothing.

Innocently, I asked, "So your father was a gold hunter in his time. Tell me, did he ever encounter any big dumplings?" In our lingo, a dumpling was a corpse that had been preserved particularly well, with no sign of decay. A *big* dumpling, well, that would mean trouble, a body that was zombified or demon-possessed, something unclean, like the creature we'd encountered up in the hills.

At these words, Gold Tooth instantly sat upright and looked at me with a great deal more respect. He asked courteously if my associate and I would like to go for a meal of boiled mut-

38

ton, his treat. He quickly packed up his cart and shepherded us to a hotpot restaurant swarming with customers. What space wasn't taken up by humanity was full of fragrant steam and the babble of different dialects.

We found an empty corner table and wedged ourselves in. As we ate, Gold Tooth opened his mouth wide and tapped on the tooth. "Young gentlemen, this gold tooth—it's white Buddha gold, plucked from a dumpling's mouth. I couldn't bear to sell it, so I kept it for myself."

What kind of thing was that to talk about halfway through a meal? Trying to change the subject, I told him about some of my grandfather's adventures, which seemed to impress him.

In turn, Gold Tooth spoke about his father and how he had relied on the Luoyang shovel to detect treasures—this was a technique that involved sticking a spade deep into the soil, pulling it out, and then sniffing it to discover what lay beneath. I joked that his father must have been a bit of an amateur. My gold-hunting ancestors wouldn't have dreamed of using anything as vulgar as a spade—they could simply glance at the ground and know what it held, particularly if the feng shui was good.

Gold Tooth listened to me prattle on. "Young master Hu," he eventually said. "I'll admit, you seem to know what you're talking about. Even at my age, I feel I've learned something from you. It's rare to meet someone so young who possesses your knowledge. What a shame you aren't putting it to good use."

He sighed and seemed to make up his mind about something. He told us he had a friend who might have a job for us—in fact, good fortune must have made us show up at his stall that day, just when this friend needed someone with our skills to help him carry out his expedition into the Taklimakan Desert. Of course, Kai and I were immediately interested. Especially when Gold Tooth explained that his friend was the legendary archaeologist Professor Chen of Peking University and that this expedition was being financed by some American millionaire. It was a chance to make my parents proud.

CHAPTER FIVE

WE ARRIVED AT THE UNIVERSITY, WHERE GOLD TOOTH SWEPT PAST the security guards and led us straight to Professor Chen's office. My first sight of the professor took me aback: he was far older than I'd expected. I had doubts that this living fossil was strong enough to head into the second-largest desert in the world.

Next to the professor was his assistant, Hao Aiguo, a typical scholar—hair as messy as a bird's nest, thick glasses perched on his nose. Gold Tooth explained why he had brought us here.

Mr. Hao sized us up. He dispensed with any polite words and launched straight in. "This is completely irregular, of course," he said. "But the fact is, we need your skills, and most of all your expertise with feng shui. If you aren't rock-solid on that point, well, there's the door." He looked directly at Gold Tooth and added, "I don't care who recommended you. How old are you boys, anyway?"

"Twenty-five," I snapped, stepping on Kai's foot to keep him quiet. "We're older than we look."

Professor Chen seemed to find his assistant's words too harsh. He'd been good friends with Gold Tooth's father, who frequently brought him artifacts to evaluate. Hastily, he stood from his sofa and tried to make amends, smiling and nodding. "It is indeed rare to find two young men who know how to cross the great Taklimakan Desert," he told us. "Bookworms like Mr. Hao and I need strapping guides like you to show the way. The thing is, what we're looking for lies buried far below the desert's yellow sands. And the Peacock River, which once flowed abundantly, dried up long ago, so we can't rely on it to trace our route. What Mr. Hao is asking is, can your feng shui knowledge help us in this regard?"

Of course I recognized what he needed—the version of feng shui known as bending the sky. I'd never actually put it into practice, but I wasn't about to tell them that. Scratching my head bashfully, I smiled ingratiatingly. "Honored Professor, I hate to boast, but you are fortunate to have found us. I don't know where I should start. . . ."

I spewed out my bellyful of knowledge, everything I remembered from the manual. I knew it inside out. Mr. Hao, who must have assumed I was some poor relative of Gold Tooth trying to bluff my way in, began to look at me in a different light.

". . . and as for the grave, it's not a simple matter of pinpointing its location. This branch of study is about the triangulation of earth, sky, and humanity."

I babbled on, describing how feng shui shows us the continuity in death of what we experienced in life, how all good and bad fortune comes straight from the dragon's veins. Our goal might be buried beneath ten centuries of sandstorms, but sky and land leave their traces, and one who knows how to read them can ferret it out.

As I completed my breathless recitation, Professor Chen leaped to his feet again, this time applauding. "Comrade Hu, well said! The heavens must have opened their eyes to our need, sending you along just at the right time. Xinjiang has indeed gone from lush green fields to desert over the last thousand years or more. The grasslands and rivers are completely gone, buried beneath the unforgiving sand, and we'd have no hope of finding these Silk Road tombs without the art of feng shui. This is the most effective way. I'd like to formally offer the two of you a place on our expedition team."

Hao Aiguo came over to shake our hands warmly, all the while apologizing. "So sorry. We academics are far too suspicious," he said. "I should never have questioned your abilities."

I said nothing, but in my head I was chuckling. It was a good thing they'd stopped me just then, as I couldn't have gone on much longer without showing how little I understood. Still, I figured with my knowledge of Grandpa's manual, I stood as good a chance of finding that tomb as anyone.

Just as I was feeling pleased with myself, a young woman walked into the room. Professor Chen rushed to introduce us. "This is Miss Yang from New York," he said. "She'll be paying the expenses for our trip. Naturally, she'll be joining us on the expedition. Although tender in years, Julie Yang is already one of National Geographic's most highly respected photographers."

I shook her hand and tried to remember how Americans greet each other. Didn't it go something like "Har . . . har . . . harloh?"

Miss Yang smiled. "Mr. Hu, I happen to know Chinese. Let's speak in your language. And please do call me Julie." Who'd have thought she'd have such good command of Mandarin, without even a trace of an accent?

Julie shook hands with Kai, then said she had a question. She'd been listening from next door and was impressed by my qualifications and my knowledge of astrology and feng shui. But she didn't see what Kai's credentials were. It was a major undertaking to venture into the desert, and she couldn't afford to carry any deadweight.

I hadn't realized Americans could be so blunt. Seeing that this girl didn't think much of him, Kai pouted. "What's so dangerous about Xinjiang?" he huffed. "When I was hunting bandits there with my dad, we shot dozens of them at Niya oasis, and I beat up the bandit chief myself. Look, this was part of my haul." With that, he pulled out his big jade amulet.

Standing beside him, I silently urged him to zip his lips. How could anyone believe his story? The incident with the Xinjiang bandits would have happened when Kai was still in diapers. The closest he'd come to that part of China was eating Xinjiang kebabs.

I was prepared to threaten not to go unless Kai came too, but Julie and Professor Chen were too busy examining his jade amulet to protest further. Their eyes followed it around the room as he brandished it, not even blinking. Gold Tooth was impressed too. "My stout young friend, this is an excellent piece, at least a thousand years old," he said. "Perhaps as early as Tang. How did you come by it?" Kai puffed up, repeating with gusto the story of his father keeping the jade piece as spoils of a Xinjiang skirmish. Not that anyone was listening to him—they were gazing closely at the carvings on the jade, which Hao Aiguo and the professor identified as Guidong— the language of the tribe we were going in search of! Just like that, Julie agreed to let Kai join the party. She promised us ten thousand American dollars each, and the same again if we managed to find the lost city of Jingjue.

Professor Chen and Julie's father had been fascinated by the tales of Jingjue City, a prosperous, magnificent metropolis, a beacon of glory in the golden age of the Western Regions. But it seemed some catastrophe had befallen the city, and after the death of its queen, Jingjue vanished altogether. The glories of the past were now buried beneath the golden sands of the desert, with only a few documents left to prove they'd even existed. Legend had it that the queen of Jingjue was the most beautiful woman in the Western Regions, and, like the sun, her appearance would diminish the stars and moon to nothing.

Julie's father had led an expedition of five Chinese and American scholars in search of this lost city. Despite having undertaken the most thorough preparations before venturing into the sea of sand, not one of them had returned. Having just turned eighteen, Julie had come into her inheritance, and was determined to use the money to retrace her father's footsteps.

Our goal was to explore and chart the ancient tomb, but

also, with any luck, to discover the bodies of those five explorers and give them a decent burial. Julie was a photographer and everyone else in the group an academic, so I somehow ended up as the expedition leader, with Kai as my deputy. It was all settled quickly.

As soon as we were a safe distance from the university, Kai and I burst into loud whoops. Gold Tooth was grinning from ear to ear. "Brilliant performance, young man. You really fooled them," he said to me.

"What do you mean?" I was a little put out. "That was all hard-earned knowledge."

"Keep that up and you'll do just fine. The eggheads just want someone there to hold their hands and keep them from getting lost. As for Miss Yang, that's a sad case. Her father was a big deal on Wall Street; archaeology was only supposed to be his hobby. Who knew he'd vanish on one expedition, not leaving a single clue, just a massive inheritance for his daughter? She might be American, but he was Chinese, and by our traditions, we bury our dead in our hometowns. Knowing her father is lying abandoned in that scorching desert—of course she wants to get him back."

"Can we talk about something more cheerful?" muttered Kai. "Or go get more food?"

Ignoring him, Gold Tooth pulled something from an inner pocket. "You two haven't been in the business long. I don't suppose you have any mojin charms, do you?" I shook my head. Charms? All I had was half an old manual.

"Look," said Gold Tooth thoughtfully, "I wouldn't normally do this, but something tells me you'll need these more than

I do." He pressed a couple of small, hard objects into my and Kai's palms. "Hang on to these mojin talismans. It kills me to let them go, but I know you'll take care of them. They were my father's."When I tried to say something, he waved away my protests. "I can't have you going out there unprotected. I'm not likely to face any undead in the middle of Beijing, but as for you . . . Besides, I won't lie—the old professor's going to give me a good fee for introducing the pair of you. This is the least I can do."

Kai and I nodded and put away our new charms next to our black donkey hooves. Hopefully, they'd keep us safe from whatever we were going to encounter—though I was personally hoping there would be nothing more threatening than some sand and perhaps the odd snake!

"Now come along," said Gold Tooth briskly. "There's a lot to be done." He led us back to the market, where we went from stall to stall, buying up all the supplies we'd need for a desert expedition. Julie Yang would be paying for it, after all, so we might as well be well equipped.

Finally, our new friend led us to an acquaintance, a stern-faced lady called Sister Han. After he explained what we wanted, she silently led us to the back of her shop, where a secret trapdoor led to a cellar full of firearms. My eyes were popping open, but I tried to look calm as I selected a couple of rifles for Kai and me, and a small handgun too. I'd borrowed my dad's police pistol for target practice with tin cans, but this was a whole different set of artillery.

"Ghosts aren't going to be scared off by bullets, are they?" Kai said, grinning. He was clearly pleased with his new toy.

"There will be more than ghosts where you're going," scolded Gold Tooth. "Bandits and wild animals, I'm sure. You must keep your guard up. The desert's a dangerous place—otherwise why wouldn't more people live there?"

A few days later, Kai and I found ourselves in our own compartment on a train speeding across the wide expanse of the Western Regions.

As my friend snored loudly, I watched the scenery whiz by, the city falling away and the countryside growing scrubby, showing signs of the desert we would soon be in. How incredible—just a week ago we'd been stuck in our village, and here we were heading for the other side of China!

Hao Aiguo stepped into our cabin and almost fainted from the stench of Kai's feet. "Comrade Hu, the professor would like to discuss a few matters with you," he told me.

I looked out the window. It was still light, but I had no idea what time it was. Throwing on my clothes, I followed Hao Aiguo to the next compartment, where Professor Chen and Julie were studying a map. They waved me to a chair, and Mr. Hao poured me a glass of water.

"Tomorrow we'll arrive at Xi'an, where three of my students will join us—the final members of our team," Professor Chen said. "Since you're the leader of this expedition, there's something I'd like to talk over with you first."

"That's right, Mr. Hu," Julie Yang added. "The professor and I are thinking we should start at Bosten Lake. From there we can head south along the bed of the old Peacock River. This should lead us deep into the desert, close to where Jingjue City might be. What do you think?"

I laughed inwardly. These academics and rich folk were good at talking, but what they were suggesting would have us walking in circles around the Gobi Desert. Their Z-shaped route was a death sentence—if thirst and heat didn't finish us off, exhaustion would. I advised them to find a local guide as soon as we arrived at Xinjiang—a far better resource than any number of maps.

At Xi'an, we met Professor Chen's archaeology students: honest-looking Sa Dipeng, tall and sturdy Chu Jian, and a young woman, Ye Yixin, whom they called Little Ye. There were now eight of us in the group.

When we arrived at Xinjiang, I phoned one of my grandfather's army friends. He was a native of the province, but he didn't know any guides. Finally, by asking around, he introduced us to an old herder who might be suitable. His name was Asahati Amati, but he went by the nickname Asat Amat, which means "living map."

Old Asat Amat, pipe dangling from his mouth, shook his head repeatedly. "No way, no way at all. It's the windy season now," he told us. "If we go into the desert, Old Hu is sure to punish us."

Old Hu—or Allah—was the god the people of the western provinces worshiped. No relation to me, of course. Trying to persuade him, I got Professor Chen to produce his documentation, which said that we were doing the government's work. Julie Yang butted in to say she was willing to buy all his livestock from him—in fact, she'd double his usual price.

Seeing he had no alternative, Asat Amat agreed, with only one request: "Don't bring any vehicles in. Old Hu doesn't like machines. Bring many, many camels. Old Hu likes camels." He warned us that the desert was most dangerous at this time of year. From here to the ruins of the Western Night City, there would be sand wastes and the Gobi Desert itself. If we couldn't find an underground water source, our fate would be uncertain.

The nine of us didn't look like an archaeological troop—more like a caravan from back in the day, burdened with a month's worth of food and ten days' water supply. There were also great leather bags of a sour-milk drink that was more refreshing than ten mouthfuls of water, and our equipment. The camels could barely manage this vast load, and we were forced to walk alongside them much of the time. As we set out from Bosten Lake, its intense blue, reaching far into the distance, was dazzling. For a moment, I felt as if we were heading toward the end of the world.

CHAPTER SIX

TWO DAYS INTO OUR EXPEDITION, THE PROFESSOR'S THREE GRADUATE students were full of high spirits. They had never been into the desert before. It was all good fun to them—learning from Asat Amat how to whistle to the camels, chasing each other as they laughed and sang. My heart was buoyant too. I would have liked to horse around, but as the expedition leader, I had to be more serious. I sat as straight as I could on my camel, trying to look stern.

The first stretch was hardly a desert at all. The Peacock riverbed wasn't completely dry, and little ponds and rivulets dotted the banks. Dark-headed gulls and scarlet-billed ducks flitted across the water's surface, and a few oases sheltered in the bend, identifiable by their date trees and shrubs.

Crossing this river would take us into the desert proper. The Peacock changed its course from here and flowed toward the southeast. We were going southwest, into the Black Desert. Asat Amat said this desert was created by Old Hu to punish greedy infidels. Countless treasures and ruined cities were hidden in the sands, but nobody would ever be able to find them and emerge alive. If you took even a single piece of gold, you'd be certain to lose your way and perish in the swirling sandstorms.

The Black Desert was a fluid place. Winds moved its dunes all the time, so the land shifted every day. There were no landmarks, and the waterways faded as soon as we set eyes on them. Fortunately, we had Asat Amat, who'd spent half his life among these yellow sands. Nothing escaped his gaze—half an ancient tower, a tree blown over nearly parallel to the ground, tiny plants. To him, these joined together in a single thread that told us the Peacock River had once flowed this way, and the legendary Jingjue City abandoned by Old Hu must be in this direction.

To avoid the noontime sun, we traveled through the night. Yet even now, as we trudged along exhausted, this scenery gave us a jolt of energy. "Gosh, this place is gorgeous," Julie Yang said with a sigh. "Look at that poplar—a golden dragon writhing through the sand." She snapped away with her camera, trying to preserve the moment.

While we were all captivated, I noticed Asat Amat staring toward the east with a glimmer of unease in his eyes. Walking over to him, I said gently, "What is it, uncle? Is the weather about to change?" I'd heard that in the inland regions, they had the saying "Red sky in the morning, travelers take warning." The rosy clouds we were admiring were probably a bad omen.

Asat Amat shook his head, pausing a little before replying, "Yes, I think the clouds in the sky are bleeding, Old Hu is throwing a tantrum, and, ah, the wind will soon rise."

I smiled. "My surname is Hu too. We Hus should stick together!"

Old Asat Amat sighed hard enough to blow a tree away. "Old Hu doesn't have a surname. He'll get angry if he hears you talking about him like that. Tonight, in the Black Desert, ah, what a wind there will be. We shouldn't rest today. Let's keep walking as fast as we can."

This was the fifth day of our expedition, and our third in the Black Desert. In front of us were the ruins of the Western Night City. We'd planned to reach them by the next day, but Asat Amat said this sandstorm would be huge. If we didn't reach the city, we'd be buried alive.

Hearing him speak like this, I realized it was no time for jokes. We were still more than half a day away from the ruins, and if there were any delays, we'd be in real trouble. But we'd just walked through the night, and the older men were beginning to tire.

I prepared to start moving again, only to see Asat Amat climb off his camel and slowly unroll a rug onto the yellow sand. Kneeling on it with his eyes shut, he raised both hands to the sky, then brought them down to his face, chanting, *"Allahu Akbar."*

Seeing Asat Amat say his prayers, as he did every morning, I began to relax. Surely it couldn't be that serious after all. My eyes moved back to the stunning desert scenery. Yet the second he finished, Asat Amat's demeanor changed completely. He leaped onto his camel as if on a giant spring and whistled loud and long. "Quick, run! Anyone too slow will be buried in the hell of the Black Desert." He spurred the camel on and began galloping away.

"Stupid old man," I cursed. To have taken his time over praying and then abandoning us like that! The other camels detected the coming peril, and their hooves clattered here and there across the sand. It's usually pleasant to sway along on the back of a camel, but in their panicked state they were giving us a much rougher ride. We clung on tightly, terrified of being flung to the ground.

The stampeding beasts raised a great pale cloud. We clapped on sand goggles and wrapped our scarves around our noses and mouths. The more I tried to work out where we were going, the more it felt wrong—the camels were out of control, their eyes bulging as they panted, trying to catch up with Asat Amat's mount, the biggest in the herd, now speeding along like a cyclone. I tried to call out to our guide, but my mouth filled with sand before I could get the words out. All I could do was count camels and riders over and over to make sure we hadn't lost anyone. We continued till noon, when even our hardy camels were foaming and in need of a rest.

Asat Amat told us to eat up and drink plenty of water— we'd be able to replenish our supplies from the underwater springs at the Western Night City. It wasn't far now, so we could allow the camels a short break, but we'd need to get moving soon.

We hastily stuffed flatbread and dried meat into our

mouths. Worried about whether these eggheads could cope with this exertion, Kai and I anxiously asked how they were.

Professor Chen was already a little frail, so the wild ride had rattled him and he couldn't answer us at first. The youngest student, Little Ye, could only stammer a few words. Neither of them was able to eat, only drink a little water.

Julie Yang was thriving. Maybe because she'd inherited her father's love of adventure, or maybe because Americans are just tougher. Whatever the reason, she wasn't looking tired at all, even after a sleepless night and a mad dash across the desert. Full of energy, she was now helping old Asat Amat check that our equipment was still securely fastened.

A light breeze blew across the dunes, raising a few wisps of sand. Looking at the horizon, we saw the sky turn a dull mustard color. Asat Amat shouted hoarsely, "The wind is here! No time to rest. Allah save us!"

The archaeologists dragged their shattered bodies back onto the camels and goaded them into action. It took no more than a breath for the clear sky to turn dark. A swift wind curled around us, carrying millions of tiny grains of sand, filling every inch of the air, reducing visibility to almost nothing. In the chaos I tried to count the galloping shapes. Eight, including myself. Who was missing?

The wind grew fiercer, the sand thicker. Now I was in the middle of a yellow blur. There was no way to see who we'd lost, but we were only a hundred yards over the crest of the dunes—there was still time to go back. Kai was by my side, the only person I could actually make out. I tried to shout at him, but there was too much wind. Instead, I gestured for him to take over and lead the group to safety. Even this little delay put us dozens of yards behind. Not stopping to see if Kai had understood me, I flipped my body off the camel and tumbled to the ground. As I ran against the wind, my body felt like a sheet of paper, as if it might be lifted and flung away at any moment. I could hear nothing but the roaring in my ears.

Stumbling a couple of hundred yards, I reached a body half covered in sand. It was Professor Chen. He looked terrible but was still breathing. The sandstorm was getting worse, but I knew this was only the beginning. I hoisted the professor onto my back and turned, only to find my footprints had already been erased. What now? With any luck, Kai would have made that cowardly Asat Amat wait.

I started down the dune, but the wind was so strong it pushed my legs out from under me, and the pair of us rolled down the slope into that strange twilight. Someone helped me up. It was Kai—he'd worked out what I was saying and rushed ahead to shove Asat Amat off his saddle. Once the lead camel came to a halt, the others did too. There they were, just in front of us. Lucky they hadn't gotten very far—we'd never have caught up otherwise.

The camels seemed spooked and refused to start running again, no matter how Asat Amat beat them. They stood in a line, knees bent, heads shoved into the sand. All along the way, I'd seen a number of camel skeletons, their bones bleached white, and always in this position. Asat Amat said they were the remains of frightened camels. Hearing the Black Desert wind coming toward them and knowing it was no use to run, they preferred to kneel and wait for death.

Unprepared for this situation, we had no plan. But we couldn't just wait to be buried alive. My mind was racing when

Julie nudged me and pointed to the west. There, looming out of the sand, was a giant white shape dashing along close to the ground. Without thinking about it, I grabbed the handgun slung from my saddle, a little revolver intended only to scare off wolves. Everyone focused on the giant white cloud. What on earth could it be?

It was almost upon us when I recognized it—a camel, twice the size of an ordinary beast, white as snow from head to tail, seeming to glow from within the swirling sand. "A wild camel!" said Asat Amat, a light in his eyes. He waved his arms and praised Allah, and the kneeling camels, seeming to sense salvation too, raised their heads. A desert creature like this would know where to hide from the sandstorm.

The camels got to their feet, lowered their heads, and ran till white foam flecked their mouths. With the last of their strength, they came close to their quarry. The land here sloped up suddenly, and the white camel's body shimmered and seemed to leap a little before vanishing.

Without stopping to work out what was happening, our little caravan pressed on until we had passed onto the other side of a high sand dune. Looking left and right, I realized the mound had a stretch of broken wall in it, a fort made of pounded earth. This had once been an ancient city. Most of it was still buried, and some buildings had crumbled altogether. After being assaulted by wind and sun, it had become the same color as the desert itself. If we hadn't approached it from just the right angle, we'd never have known it was here.

The white camel had been heading to this spot to shelter from the storm. Only the broken wall had prevented us from seeing exactly where it was going. This wall must have been designed to keep out the harsh desert. Asat Amat said, "We were directed here by Old Hu." True, a safe haven like this felt like divine providence.

The archaeologists clustered together, their faces yellow—though whether from fear or because covered with sand I couldn't tell. Asat Amat stabled the camels in a corner, then led the rest of us into a large building that still had some of its roof intact.

This city must have been solid in its day, but now the walls were cracked open in places, and over time huge quantities of sand had drifted into its structures. Looking around, I saw that we seemed to be in some kind of public hall—a courtroom or maybe some other meeting place.

Little Ye and Hao Aiguo flung themselves to the ground as soon as they came in, pouring water from their bottles into their mouths. The rest of us helped Professor Chen inside. He had recovered somewhat, but his legs were still wobbly.

Asat Amat came in last. He knelt to thank Old Hu for sending the white camel that had led us from the nightmare of the dark demons raised by the Black Desert. The single-humped white camel, he said, was one of the mysteries of the desert. Genghis Khan had reported sighting one. Our whole group must be favored by Allah, for if Old Hu didn't approve of a single person among us, he'd never have sent it. From now on we would be Asat Amat's brothers and sisters, bound together. He puffed out his chest and proclaimed, "If there's any more danger, I promise never again to abandon you to save my own skin!"

The great sandstorm arrived while Asat Amat was speaking, the furious winds seeming to shake the very ground. Even within the walls of our sanctuary, we were terrified. What if sand blocked the entrance and turned this building into our mausoleum? Kai, Sa Dipeng, and Chu Jian took turns keeping an eye on the crack we'd crawled in through, ready to raise the alarm if it started to fill up. Yet we knew deep down there was nothing we could do. Even if we fled, we'd be running into the maw of the storm—just choosing a different location in which to be buried alive.

The outer walls of this hall were overgrown with sand wormwood, a kind of dry grass. I reached out to harvest an armful for kindling—fire would give us a little warmth and illuminate the pitch-black interior. Little Ye suddenly leaped up, hitting her head on a ceiling beam and knocking clouds of sand down on us. Before my vision cleared, I heard her shaking voice: "Over there, look—a body!"

"A corpse?" Hao Aiguo was scornful. "Silly Little Ye, what's the big deal? Since when have archaeologists been afraid of the dead?"

Little Ye rubbed her head where it had hit the beam. "I'm sorry, Teacher Hao, I—I never expected to see one here. I wasn't prepared."

Everyone else on the team except Asat Amat had seen their share of corpses, so no one seemed as alarmed as Little Ye. Rather, they were curious—bodies usually became mummified in the heat and drying winds of the desert, yet there wasn't a shred of skin or flesh left on this skeleton. Had the bones been eaten clean by sand wolves?

Asat Amat thought that was possible. Since the white camel had led us here to shelter from the storm, the ruins were likely a sanctuary provided by Old Hu for the creatures of the desert. Who knew how many sand leopards and yellow sheep were hiding among the buildings, just out of our sight? When the storm cleared, the chase of predator and prey could start up again.

At the thought of sharing our shelter with possibly vicious wild creatures, Little Ye began to panic again. Asat Amat grew anxious too, going out to make sure the camels were where he'd left them. Kai and Chu Jian accompanied him, planning to bring the food and sleeping bags back in case we were stuck here for a while. The three squeezed through the hole in the roof, sand goggles and scarves shielding them. Teacher Hao paced nervously, first in one direction, then in the other. Before he could start a second go-round, Kai and Chu Jian were back, their bodies covered in grit.

Kai stripped off his protective gear. "That wind! If we hadn't held on to each other, we'd have been blown away," he said. "But the old guy wasn't bluffing: we saw six or seven sheep huddled behind a wall. When it calms down, I'll go shoot a couple. It's been too long since I've tasted fresh meat."

Asat Amat overheard and rushed to stop him. "Cannot, cannot do this. If you shoot, the noise will scare all the other animals here. They'll rush out into the Black Desert and be buried alive. They're Old Hu's creatures, just like us."

Kai sighed. "Fine, don't get bent out of shape. I'll stick to the dried meat. Or does Old Hu object to that too?"

Trapped in this nameless ancient city after so many days in the desert, no one had much of an appetite. I was worried about Professor Chen—what if something happened to him, so far from any medical help? We had a skinful of brandy, which I pressed on him. After sipping it, he smiled weakly. "To think I used to work in the field every day. Now I'm just old and useless. Little brother Hu, if it weren't for you, my old bones would be buried in that desert."

I tried to comfort him and joked that I had to do some work in exchange for Miss Yang's generous wages. If he wasn't feeling well, it wasn't too late to turn back; beyond the Western Night City would be the heart of the Black Desert, where conditions would be much worse and there would be no time for second thoughts.

The professor shook his head, indicating he was determined to carry on. Big sandstorms only came along once a century, and he was certain we wouldn't encounter anything else of this magnitude. As long as we got through this, there could only be good fortune in store.

After dinner, it was Sa Dipeng's turn to relieve Chu Jian. Kai and I went to retrieve the bones Little Ye had spotted earlier. There was no way to bury them outside, so we picked a spot inside the building. After a few strokes, the shovel struck something hard, which was strange. This tall building was filled with centuries of blowing sand. How could we have hit rock so soon?

Probing a little farther, we found a round object. Teacher Hao and the others came to help, and soon we'd created a hole almost two feet deep. From out of the powdery sand, there now protruded a human head carved out of black stone. Bulging olive-shaped eyes were set into its proportionately smaller features. The head wore no hat, only an ornate hairpin, and its expression was as calm and detached as that of a temple statue.

I lit a gas lamp. Staring at the head in the light, Professor Chen said to Hao Aiguo, "Look at this. Haven't we seen something like it before?"

Hao Aiguo put on his glasses and studied it. "Yes, that thousand-tomb site in Xinjiang? There were stone figures like this on those graves."

I chose another spot and quickly dug a hole, and finally, that unfortunate skeleton was buried. Not a shred of clothing or other identifying object was left. Who was he? Knowing nothing about him, I just murmured, "Rest in peace."

CHAPTER SEVEN

IT WAS EVENING, AND STILL THE BLACK DESERT STORM WAS CHURNING away outside. I worried it would continue all night.

Apart from Sa Dipeng, who was on sentry duty, everyone had cleaned their feet with sand—a trick learned from Asat Amat—and was now sound asleep, cocooned in sleeping bags. I told Dipeng to get some rest. Sitting with my back against a wall, I cradled my rifle and kept a sharp lookout for wild animals that might be thinking of attacking as we slept. How much deeper into the Black Desert would we be going, and what traps lay in wait for us?

This is how the desert is—calm on the surface, especially when there's no wind; a world covered in fine gold dust. But this smooth exterior has swallowed countless beasts, countless people. The ever-changing dunes and the creatures that live among them are all potential threats. Danger lurks everywhere. It was a miracle not to have lost Professor Chen or any member of our team.

Sunk in thought, I didn't notice that the sky had gradually darkened. The wind was unabated, like the sobs of countless demons. Now and then, sand trickled through cracks in the roof. If this went on much longer, the wall we'd climbed through would be completely submerged.

A movement caught my eye. It was Julie Yang, walking toward me. I hadn't spoken to her very much, mainly because she and Kai didn't get along—in fact, as the days went by, they seemed unable to stand each other. To be polite, I smiled at her. Julie said, "Mr. Hu, you should get some sleep. I'll stand guard for a couple of hours." I told her there was no need, that Mr. Wang would be taking over soon. Instead of going back to sleep, she came and sat beside me.

There was something I'd been meaning to ask her: "Miss Yang, why is it so important to find this ancient city of Jingjue? How do you know there is any trace of it left? No one has ever discovered its location—your father and his team could have ended up anywhere. Deserts all contain untold dangers, and this one is an unsolved riddle."

Julie nodded. "Mr. Hu, what you say makes sense, but I've always believed my father found Jingjue City," she said. "From the time he went missing, I've dreamed of a huge gaping hole, dark as lacquer. A coffin hangs above it, tightly wrapped in chains. Something gigantic is perched on top of it, but I can't quite make out the shape. Each time I peer closely, I always wake up just before the shape comes into focus. It's been more than six months now, and I've had this dream almost every night. I'm certain it's a vision sent by my father, and that the coffin belongs to the queen of Jingjue."

Who'd have thought Americans could be this superstitious? Not daring to question her, I placed a comforting arm around her shoulder and asked what she knew about the queen.

"My father migrated to America early on," she said. "He bought a trunk of historical documents in the States. It had been discovered by some European archaeologists in Xinjiang at Niya oasis, near some ruins that they were able to prove dated from the Han dynasty. All this pointed to Jingjue City, the most powerful of the thirty-six kingdoms of the Western Regions. He got an expedition together and ventured into the desert. All his life, he'd been drawn to the story of this glittering ancient place. We wouldn't even know of its existence if it weren't for a British explorer who led a group into the Taklimakan Desert before World War Two. He was the only one to emerge alive, though his sanity was long gone. The evidence of his camera and diaries showed remnants of Jingjue."

Julie handed me a package. I unwrapped it to find some yellowing black-and-white photographs and an old notebook crammed full of English words. The pictures were hazy, but I could make out some kind of desert settlement with a spire in its center.

Julie answered my questioning look: "Yes, this is what my father brought back from England. They belong to the unfortunate explorer. His diary only records what happened up to the point when he reached the underground river leading to the city. He says something about entering its walls the next morning—and then it goes blank."

As we continued to talk, I thought I saw a movement from the corner where the great stone head was. One of its eyes had twitched. Could this be happening? Or was I seeing things after two nights in a row without sleep?

I walked over to investigate. The gas lamps were shaking in the wind, dappling the walls with light and dark stripes. As I drew closer, I realized the culprit was a huge black ant, the size of a knuckle joint, creeping across the eye. Its tail segment was a smear of red, and it was this that caught the light. I flicked the insect to the ground and stepped on it. Strange; it was harder than any ant had a right to be.

The walls were full of cracks—it was difficult to say which one the ant had used as its entrance. Julie came over to see if I was all right and I said it was nothing, just an ant. I woke Kai for his turn as sentry, added some fuel to the fire, and turned off the gas lamp before burrowing into my sleeping bag. I was so exhausted that it seemed only moments before morning arrived, still roaring with wind, though a little less forcefully than the night before. Maybe this demonic storm was finally coming to an end.

Yet more sand had blown over the ruin, and barely any of its surface could be seen. A couple more storms like this and the city might vanish altogether—though not forever, because the endlessly stirring sands of the Taklimakan ebbed and flowed and might spit forth these ruins again.

Hao Aiguo and his students had excavated more of the statue, all the way down to its thighs. The whole team was clustered around the site except Asat Amat, who was taking advantage of the weakening wind to check on his camels.

Pulling more dried food from my pack, I watched blearily as they worked. Afraid of damaging the carvings on the stone body, they were proceeding gingerly, using a fine brush to dust the sand off. Professor Chen nodded a greeting at me. He seemed to have recovered. This would be a chance for the students to get some practical experience, he told me—much more important than any amount of book learning.

Before long, the whole statue stood revealed before us. It was dressed in the style of the Hu tribe——a long robe tied with a sash, over a wide skirt——arms by its side, torso covered with markings that appeared to be some kind of religious text. Professor Chen recognized the language as undecipherable. No one was even sure whether it consisted of words or some sort of code.

Sa Dipeng interrupted to ask, "Professor, this statue is much bigger than others like it. I wonder if this tribe could have been visited by extraterrestrials. They could have mistaken the aliens for gods and built idols to worship them. These marks could be the language of another planet."

"You should study harder, Sa, my boy," scolded Hao Aiguo. "You're a bright fellow, but your brains are all over the place. How did you leap from here to aliens?"

The professor, in contrast, smiled kindly. "It's no bad thing to have imagination, young man. It keeps the brain active. But as archaeologists working with history, we have to follow one principle: hypothesize boldly, but investigate cautiously. Creativity has to be based on a foundation of facts. Take this big-eyed statue as an example. The ancients thought their destinies were written in the sky and studied the stars for answers. Wouldn't they have wished their eyes could see a little farther? And mightn't they have expressed this wish through the figures they carved?

Similar ones have been found in Sichuan's Three Stars Mound. I'd wager they show the aspirations of our ancestors."

I let out my breath in admiration at Professor Chen's profound knowledge. He had shared what he knew without trying to crush his listeners' own intelligence. Hopefully, Hao Aiguo would learn a thing or two from this.

Asat Amat burst in just then to say he believed the storm would be over within half an hour, thanks to Allah's intervention. Sand had almost covered the exterior wall; if the wind had lasted just a couple of hours more, we'd certainly have been buried alive.

The team, anxious despite the diminishing wind, were able to relax at Asat Amat's words. The students continued to listen to Professor Chen's wisdom, and I put a kettle on the fire to boil. We'd be able to start moving once we'd had our tea.

Just as steam started rising from the spout, screams erupted near the statue. I saw the others running back and forth, calling out, "Where are they coming from?" and "Oh God, there are more over there!" Dashing over to look, I saw a bubble of sand rising, spewing forth countless huge ants. Chu Jian was whacking away with a shovel, but even though he must have swatted hundreds of them, he didn't seem to put a dent in their numbers. They continued to swarm out, packed so densely it made my scalp itch to look at them.

I thought we must have disturbed a nest with our digging but looking around, I saw dozens of holes opening up across the room, floods of ants rising from them, all the insects like the one I'd seen the night before—shiny black bodies, a crimson rear. Asat Amat took one glance and fled straight back out.

Chu Jian abandoned his shovel—there were just too many ants for him to make a difference.

Julie, having seen more of the world than most of us in her work as a photographer, knew immediately what was going on. "Everyone, quick, on the roof!" she cried. "These are desert army ants—if you're too slow, they'll eat your flesh and leave nothing but bones."

The ants seemed to take up half the space in the room now, more arriving every second. Not just on the floor, but also on the walls and pillars, climbing everywhere. Little Ye whimpered as she took hesitant steps back and forth, but there was no way to avoid them.

Never mind the eggheads, even Kai and I were trembling. These tiny insects looked terrifyingly vicious. Could the skeleton we'd found earlier have been one of their victims? No wonder not even the slightest scrap of flesh was left.

I tried hard to calm myself down. Asat Amat, for all his promises to protect us, was long gone. No time to curse that slippery coward. I tipped over the fire and scattered solid fuel in front of us. Soon a wall of fire shielded us, but the ants seemed willing to hurl themselves into the flames, and as more charred bodies piled up, I realized it was only a matter of time before they snuffed it out.

We used the few minutes we had to pack up our equipment as well as we could, hauling it up to the roof. By now the sandstorm had waned to almost nothing. It was chaos below us—dozens of yellow sheep, wild camels, sand wolves, and mice were stampeding through the ruins of the city. The army ants were out here too, swarming over any animal that moved too slowly. With the venom in their jaws, Julie hastily explained to us, they could stop the heart of an elephant.

There must have been millions of the black and red creatures. Had the ruins somehow become a giant nest? We used our shovels to keep them from getting too close. Meanwhile, by the far wall, Asat Amat was fumbling with his camels' ropes, trying to untie them so he could make his escape. I tossed my rifle to Kai and said, "Hit his hat."

Kai aimed and fired without hesitation, and with a bang Asat Amat's leather cap went flying. "Old man, don't you dare run," I yelled. "Or the next bullet will hit your backside, and I don't think Old Hu will mind."

Asat Amat waved his hands frantically in surrender. Although our rides were secure, we still couldn't get across to them. Staying on the roof wasn't an option either—as we watched, a nearby wall collapsed, and out of the wreckage climbed an ant the size of a small calf. This must be the queen—her torso had six pairs of transparent wings sprouting from it. Had the sandstorm disturbed the whole colony, prompting the queen to lead a migration?

The appearance of the gigantic insect made us all go pale. Julie shouted, "Strike the head to kill the body. Shoot her!"

Kai stamped his feet with agitation. "That won't do any good!" he yelled. "My rifle isn't powerful enough!" He fired anyway, emptying his magazine, but sure enough, the queen was unharmed.

I pulled off my scarf and wrapped the remaining solid fuel in it, lit one corner, and, timing it carefully, dropped it off the roof onto the giant insect. The queen writhed as she sizzled, and her soldiers swarmed toward her, frantically trying to smother the flames with their bodies. I saw our chance and waved for everyone to leap off the roof. Tall Chu Jian carried Professor Chen on his back. The rest followed single file, with Kai bringing up the rear.

Asat Amat had calmed the camels down by now, and we were able to scramble onto them, heading for the open desert. Wild animals of all kinds surged past us, but the predators among them were no threat. Like us, they just wanted to escape.

I turned back after a few hundred yards, by which time the walls of the city were more or less gone, covered by a bubbling mass of red and black bodies, churning like the sea. They weren't leaving the ruins, though; we were safe now.

Groveling, Asat Amat explained that he hadn't intended to abandon us, he was only trying to lead the camels away before the ants reduced them to skeletons. Kai didn't believe him, tapping his rifle and growling, "Tell it to my gun." I put my hand on his shoulder—we couldn't afford to quarrel with Asat Amat; we needed him to get us out alive.

"We found refuge, thanks to the white camel, and then escaped the army of ants," I said. "It must have been through Old Hu's intervention, which means he favors us. We're your brothers, Asat Amat, and trust in you. Old Hu will surely punish anyone who betrays a brother."

Asat Amat was pleased. Over and over he said, "Praise Allah, Old Hu is the one true god. We're all brothers, friends and brothers. The true lord will surely protect us."

And so we survived another calamity and pressed on, the nine of us and our camels trekking across that wide expanse, insignificant as so many grains of sand.

CHAPTER EIGHT

WE WERE STILL HALF A DAY'S JOURNEY FROM THE WESTERN NIGHT City when the wind finally died down. Instead of traveling under a blanket of stars, we'd been traveling by day, under a blazing sun. We did so only because we had more than enough water to stay hydrated, and because we would be able to replenish our supplies at our destination.

The desert was featureless and borderless in all directions. If not for the long trail of footprints behind us, we'd scarcely have believed we were moving forward at all. I felt a burst of respect for those solo explorers who ventured into the Gobi. Maybe only by walking alone between heaven and earth could they truly understand the meaning of life. Of course, as much as I admired them, I'd never do such a thing in my life—I'm someone who needs to be around others.

I noticed that the sand beneath our feet was rising and falling much more than before. Asat Amat told us that under these tightly packed dunes was an ancient city swallowed by the yellow sand. He asked everyone to climb up to the highest peak and, pointing to the south, informed us that our destination was straight ahead: the ruins of the Western Night City.

I raised my binoculars for a closer look. A lush green oasis filled my vision, like an emerald on a tray of golden sand, with the dark ruins of a city in its center.

The Western Night City was well preserved. It had been founded relatively late and wasn't destroyed until the wars of the late Tang dynasty. At the start of the nineteenth century, a German expedition discovered it and made off with most of the paintings and statues, anything of cultural value.

Now only this shell of a city was left in the desert, and the ancient Peacock River petered out here. Because underground water channels crossed this point throughout the year, it had become a crucial site for desert travelers to replenish their supplies.

As the line of camels descended the large dune toward the distant green, Asat Amat suggested that we rest a couple of days there before entering the Black Desert, after which it would be hard to turn back. Our pack animals had been through a great deal and needed to be fully recovered before setting off again, given how important their cargo was.

This sounded good to me. I welcomed the break and thought I might find some excuse to get the team to turn around. Forget about finding Jingjue City; just dig a couple of pits nearby and be done with it. The longer this expedition went on, the less my heart was in it, and I thought the more time we spent in the desert, the more likely it was that something would go wrong. Next time we might not be so lucky.

The greenery hadn't looked too far away from the top of the dune, but it took a solid three hours' walking before we arrived there. The city walls were made of black stone, badly weathered in some places, though the citadel itself was solidly built and showing traces of its former glory. Whenever oil field workers, archaeologists, or geological surveyors passed through, they always sought refuge here, blocking the entrances with rocks to keep wolves out.

It was the middle of the windy season, so no one was likely to come by except us. We found a spacious room in the citadel, lit a campfire, and started making food.

Asat Amat and I went in search of the city's ancient well, which allegedly hadn't run dry once in thousands of years. Asat Amat assured me this was a miracle from Old Hu, which I chose not to comment on. When we found the well, we lowered a bucket. The shaft was deep, and we didn't hear a splash until several dozen yards of rope had passed through our hands. I pulled the bucket up and took the first sip. The water was icy cold, so pure and refreshing that the desert heat vanished in an instant.

We brought all nineteen camels over to the well and watered them thoroughly, then set out the salt licks and bean cakes that were their food. Only after the animals were taken care of did we return to where the archaeologists were resting, with two buckets of well water.

Everyone was wiped out, collapsed on the ground fast asleep, some even with half a biscuit between their teeth, so tired they'd fallen asleep halfway through their meal. I let them doze a little longer, only waking them when I'd boiled a pot of water, instructing everyone to wash their feet and then pop any blisters that had formed.

When all that was done, I could finally sleep, and must have been dead to the world through an entire day and night before my body recovered. The second night, we sat around the fire as Kai entertained us.

He was quite the storyteller, regaling the crowd with tales of how good life was in the northeast, with so many delicious things to eat—not like this desert, which had only sand and more sand, and even if you shot a goat and cooked it, you'd probably find a grain of sand in every mouthful. Where we came from, there was such abundance, you could hold out a club and a deer would run into it; birds flew straight into your cooking pot. Just imagine what a blissfully free life that was.

The students were mostly city slickers who ate up that garbage. Julie humphed and said, "The desert has plenty of good things too, not to mention just as many varieties of plants and animals as the forest. And the Taklimakan Valley might be the lowest point of the basin, but you could also call it the peak of ancient civilization. What do your woods have, except deer and bears?"

I worried they were going to start fighting, so I quickly asked Kai to come check the perimeter with me. Outside, the moon looked like something from a painting, and there were so many stars everything was covered in silvery light.

"Go easy on Julie," I told him.

"Easy? She thinks she's better than us. If she weren't a girl, I'd have ripped off her head and used it as a football already."

I smiled. "Okay, you don't have to like her, but please don't rip her head off. I want her to be around to pay our wages. Twenty thousand American dollars! Think about it!"

I tilted my head back to look at the sky, which was brilliantly clear. Suddenly, I noticed the Vast Door star in the center, the Left Auxiliary star and the Right Guardian star gleaming brightly in a right-angled triangle. In its center were the sun star and the moon star, side by side. Such a perfect alignment couldn't be a coincidence.

I'd never dabbled in astrological feng shui before, but for the sake of this expedition, I would have to learn very quickly. Even looking up at it now, all the secrets from the ancient book flashed up in my mind, superimposing themselves upon the night sky.

I ran back to my rucksack and got my compass, then hurried again to the roof to triangulate the stars. Sure enough, the good-fortune ones were all focused on that ancient well. This was my first practical attempt at doing this, and while I felt uncertain, I thought I'd probably gotten it right. *The Sixteen Mysteries of Yin-Yang Feng Shui* was no ordinary book, and I was sure I'd followed its rules precisely. So did that mean the ancient graves were here? Some people do say that tombs should be near water.

Professor Chen was delighted at the news. He and his students rushed to the well and clamored to go down and have a look. I talked it over with Julie, and we decided that someone could be lowered down the deep shaft on a double harness.

That someone could only be me. No room for carelessness—I strapped on my gas mask and made sure I had a flashlight, whistle, military surplus spade, and knife, then secretly slipped my black donkey hoof and gold-hunter's talisman into a pocket. Making sure the rope was taut, I told the others my signal: I would flash my light in a circle three times. The first time I did that, they would stop lowering me, and the second time they'd pull me up. The whistle would be a backup, in case the well was too deep for the flashlight to be seen.

As I descended, the mouth of the well grew murky, and soon I was in a glowing bubble surrounded by pitch darkness. The desert temperature drops at night, and in the damp of the well, the cold seemed to penetrate my bones. The walls were too slippery to get a grip on. It was said that this well was even older than the city itself—that the citadel had been built around it. A freezing gust of air blasted me. I swung my flashlight toward it and saw a stone door set into the shaft.

Shining the light above me, I blew my whistle for good measure. I hadn't gone down that far, maybe fifty feet or so; they could probably have heard me if I'd shouted. The rope stopped, leaving me right at the level of the door. The icy wind was coming from the cracks around it. I pushed hard. It felt heavy and thick, and there was no lock of any kind, yet it wouldn't budge. It would have to be pried open.

I signaled again to be pulled up, then told the others what I'd seen. Professor Chen was intrigued. "Strange. It could be that this isn't a mausoleum, but some sort of secret passage. No one would build a tomb into the side of a well."

Kai stepped forward and blustered, "What's the use in guessing? Let's see for ourselves. I'll go down and smash that door in."

"Why don't I do it?" I suggested. "You're so heavy the rope might snap."

This time we made a rope ladder so the others could come down after I'd gotten the door open. We decided that the professor, Julie, and Sa Dipeng would follow me, while Kai and the others would stay up top.

I went first, crowbar at the ready. The door must have been in frequent use at one point—its frame was heavily scuffed—but after staying shut for centuries, it required a fair bit of effort to get it open again, especially as I was swinging from a rope and couldn't get much leverage.

Behind the door was a brick tunnel, sturdily built and spacious, stretching into inky darkness. I called up for the other three to come, and soon we were standing in the tunnel. Julie gave us all pills to prevent oxygen deprivation, and we strapped on our gas masks.

Passing through another two doors, we made it fifty yards down the passage before reaching a final one, sealed tight, inscribed with some strange animal and sealed with animal skin. We had to chip the leathery skin off piece by piece before the door would open.

Behind it was a stone room, maybe twenty feet wide and ten feet high. The four of us could stand in it without feeling cramped. Despite the generous proportions, the place felt stifling. White bones littered the floor. They looked like animal bones, and they were so fragile they splintered as soon as our feet touched them. In all four corners were dozens of wooden poles, from which hung desiccated human bodies, all young men, from the looks of them.

Julie, the professor, and I were used to this sort of thing, but Sa Dipeng was so terrified at the sight of the corpses that he couldn't speak. He stood close to the professor and followed him when he moved, not daring to be on his own.

Julie examined one of the bodies. "How awful. These must have been slaves or prisoners," she said, sighing. "Barbaric."

Professor Chen agreed. "This looks like an important figure's funeral ritual. In ancient Gumo, it was the custom to bring criminals out into the desert and tie them up till they died of thirst and all the moisture left their corpses. Then the wind-dried bodies were strung up here, smeared with blood from slaughtered animals. Let's have a look—the actual tomb must be nearby."

We explored, tapping on the stone walls—all solid— trying to find the hidden space. It was Julie who noticed something odd about the floor. I swept aside the bone fragments, and sure enough, a large stone slab covered in carvings was revealed, metal rings at either end.

I called Sa Dipeng over to help me lift it, but his whole body was trembling so hard he couldn't. Trying not to laugh, I told him to go back up and send Hao Aiguo down instead. Looking relieved, he fled. As soon as he'd left, Professor Chen muttered, "That boy. No guts. He'll never make an archaeologist."

Julie and I lifted the stone slab and tossed a flare down. In the glow, we saw a chamber about the size of the one we were in, with an unusual coffin right in its center—it was perfectly square and had no carvings on it at all. I'd never seen anything like it, and even Professor Chen with all his learning couldn't shed any light on the matter.

Hao Aiguo showed up, his eyes glowing at the sight. He

was the first to leap into the pit, darting everywhere, clearly overjoyed. Up till now, I'd thought of him as a fusty old scholar, but he suddenly seemed like a little child. He was so excited he was almost dancing.

The rest of us climbed down too, and we all exclaimed at what we saw: the four walls of the vault were covered with dazzling, delicate paintings. Professor Chen zeroed in on one of them. "Look here—this is the Jingjue Kingdom," he told us.

I was most interested in the valuable grave goods—such a large coffin must hold quite a few good things. Of course, I wasn't about to start grave robbing in front of the professor and the others, but I was eager to take a look. Already I was hoping this aristocrat's tomb would be at least as richly laden as the one in the Liao caves. Yet the professor seemed determined to ignore the coffin, focusing on those drawings instead, so I had to listen patiently as he and Hao Aiguo discussed them.

The first few in the series made it clear that the tomb belonged to a Gumo prince—Gumo being one of Jingjue's vassal states, which meant its residents were forced to give Jingjue large amounts of treasure, cattle, and slaves every year. The prince had gone to see the queen of Jingjue, pleading for the freedom of his people, but after three visits, he hadn't seen her face once. Being the reincarnation of a sun god, the prince wasn't going to put up with that. He sneaked back alone into Jingjue, determined to murder the evil queen—but then he discovered a secret.

Despite myself, I got sucked into the professor's story and went closer to listen. Professor Chen walked over to the next panel and stared at it for a long time. "The meaning of this one is odd," he said. "Look, the prince is hiding in a corner, peering out. In all the pictures so far, the queen's face has been covered with a veil. In this one, we see her from behind as she raises a hand to lift the veil, and another figure over there—a slave, perhaps?—turns into a wisp of shadow and disappears."

Confused, I was going to ask him to explain, when Julie blurted out, "So the queen is a demon?"

"A demon?" the professor repeated, seeming more intrigued than surprised. "Interesting. Go on."

Julie gestured at the murals. "These paintings are all extremely well executed, both artistically and as a form of storytelling. Even without words, they tell the story of this Gumo prince very clearly."

I looked closely, and it was as she said. The facial expressions and clothing, the buildings, everything was finely detailed. With even the slightest knowledge of the Western Regions, you'd quickly be able to grasp what was going on.

"The panel the professor was just talking about is the hardest to understand," Julie continued. "The queen is removing her veil, and the person she's facing is drawn with a blurry outline. Everyone else is clearly drawn, while he or she is reduced to a faint silhouette. We don't know who this is—whether it's an assassin, or whether the queen herself is eliminating an enemy."

"Miss Yang," I asked, "do you mean that the sight of this woman's face could cause a person to vanish?"

"More or less. Or rather, I believe it was anyone she looked at directly."

I shook my head. "A whole, living person, disappearing with a single look? That's . . . that's not possible."

The professor seemed to see where Julie was going with this, and nodded at her to continue.

"I don't have any evidence, but this isn't a blind guess. When my father was alive, he often read a book called *Great Tang Records of the Western Regions* by the Buddhist monk Xuanzang. I've read it a few times. It's a compendium of ancient legends from this part of China, mixed in with real incidents. One story talks about a city deep within the desert, inhabited by a tribe from underground that conquered all its neighboring states. After several centuries, the throne passed to a woman, and it was said that her eyes were a direct gateway to the underworld. She only had to glance at an enemy for him to vanish without a trace, never to return. As for where these unfortunate souls ended up, only they could know. She was a tyrant, demanding to be worshiped as a goddess. Anyone who refused was skinned alive. Perhaps her actions displeased some higher power, because a few years later, she caught a mysterious disease and died.

"The queen's slaves feared her more than anyone else. When she perished, they joined forces with the neighboring states that she'd had under her thumb, and washed her kingdom with blood. Just as they were about to desecrate her tomb, the sky changed color, and a fearsome sandstorm swallowed both them and the entire city. The queen's grave, and the countless treasures she'd amassed, were buried beneath the golden sands for centuries, until the dunes shifted and the city came to light once more. A few travelers stumbled upon it, but anyone who tried to take even the smallest item found themselves assaulted by strong winds and thick clouds of sand, leaving them completely lost. No one who tried to steal her possessions was ever able to leave this place.

"There's been no record of where this mysterious kingdom with its evil queen might actually have existed. But seeing these pictures today, I think there are too many similarities to the legend for it not to be connected. And it could be that this was no legend but a retelling of actual historical events."

Julie pointed at the next few pictures. "We can be sure this is the queen because of her clothing and the buildings behind her, both of which are in the unique Jingjue style. Professor, look at what comes next and you'll see that my hypothesis has to be right. It's very clear what happened—the prince failed in his assassination attempt, so he returned home and continued plotting against the queen. Then a mystic from a distant land arrived and told the prince to put a specially made slow-acting poison into the meat of a golden goat, which he should then offer to the queen. The prince did as he suggested and soon heard the news of the queen's sudden death. Not long after that, the prince died too, of exhaustion. He was buried with his beloved wife. The mystic laid out their tomb, arranging for them to rest beneath the altar of the sacred well."

So the altar above us had existed before this vault. The story on these walls dovetailed exactly with the one in Julie's book. The professor looked at her differently now, as if realizing she wasn't just a photographer, but had also inherited the scholarship of her archaeologist father. Thinking of his old friend, lost in the desert, a tear came to his eye.

"Don't be sad. We've done well—this will help us understand a great deal more about Jingjue," Julie said to him. "I'm sure we'll find the ancient city before too long. My father's watching over us, I know."

I cursed myself. Instead of satisfying them enough to stop the journey, this discovery had made them more determined than ever to keep going. If I'd known this would happen, I'd have kept quiet about the stone door.

Suddenly remembering something, I turned to Julie. "Miss Yang, earlier you said that the queen was the most beautiful woman in all of the Western Regions, and all the other ladies faded before her like stars before the sun. How could you also say she's a demon? And if she really is one, aren't we asking for trouble by looking for her tomb?"

"That's a legend," replied Julie. "And I've added my own deductions to it, but it's still not a fact. That's how archaeology works: it's a mixture of mythology, records, artifacts, and some informed guesswork. The more data we have, the closer we get to the historical truth—but all we can ever do is get closer and closer to it. History will never be captured completely. In ancient times, people knew very little about the world, and some things that seem commonplace to us would have appeared demonic or divine to them. Even though we're more advanced, there are still things we can't explain with science. I don't think ghosts and demons actually exist; they're just phenomena that we aren't yet scientifically advanced enough to understand."

"So how can we explain the queen making people disappear just by looking at them?"

"There was a case a few years ago in Kansas, a state in America," she said. "A twelve-year-old boy had the strange ability to make tiny objects vanish in thin air if he stared directly at them. His neighbors thought he was a monster. His parents were worried too, so they asked the government doctors to cure him."

I'd never heard about this, but I don't even know much about what's happening here in China, never mind all the way over in America.

"Scientists studied the boy," Julie continued, "and discovered that his brain waves were somehow able to combine with his visual nerves to teleport objects by creating a connection to a parallel dimension. Only one in three billion people have this power. Finally, a researcher fixed a magnetic helmet onto the boy's head, and within a year he'd lost this ability. The US Army tried to detain the boy to study his brain, but there was a public outcry and it was forced to drop its plan."

This story didn't reassure me at all. I wasn't afraid of dying, but what if we got to the evil queen's tomb and we found ourselves getting zapped into some parallel dimension? I decided to stay alert and to force a retreat at the first sign of danger. I didn't think these scholars would dare go against me if I insisted.

After all that talk, we seemed to have finally exhausted the topic of the wall paintings. This seemed like a good moment for me to respectfully turn to the professor and ask if he'd like to take a look inside the coffin.

Professor Chen batted the suggestion away. "Absolutely not! This is the Gumo prince and his consort's grave, a national treasure," he said firmly. "We don't have the right equipment. If we broke the seal, the coffin and its contents would start to deteriorate. The only course of action is to inform the authorities and apply for permission to excavate the tomb, or better yet, for it to receive formal protection. Aiguo will take all the evidence we need, and I'll write the report myself."

It seemed I wouldn't be getting a look at the contents of this coffin. I knew the professor was right, but I couldn't help feeling disappointed. No alternative now but to climb back up into the altar room with the rest of them.

According to the professor, the animal skins sealing the door were there to keep out the moisture of the well, preserving the dry atmosphere. We had no way of replacing them, seeing as there were no large animals around apart from the camels, which we weren't about to start slaughtering. In the end, we shut the door and covered the cracks with layers of tape, hoping that would do the job.

CHAPTER NINE

Our team rested in the Western Night City for three days before setting off for the north, into that stretch of sand known as the Black Desert. Here there were no desert poplars, and the sand didn't rise and fall in dunes but lay flat as a steamed bun, looking exactly the same from every angle, no sign of life in any direction.

I asked Asat Amat if he'd ever been through this stretch before. He smiled grimly. "These sands are hell on earth—Old Hu himself wouldn't dare to come here," he answered. "As for me, I've only been here once in this life, and that's right now. If the old man hadn't insisted, if Old Hu hadn't shown the way with the white camel, I'd rather die than set foot here."

He might grumble a lot, but Asat Amat lived up to his

reputation for being a living map. He knew every inch of this place. Even though it was his first time in the Black Desert, he had the eyes of a desert fox and was able to spot the few wisps of vegetation amid the sand, sedge grass, and sagebrush. Only by following this faint trail of life was he able to lead the expedition into this treacherous land.

Over the course of many ruling dynasties—Han, Yuan, Ming—the desert eroded the green spaces and the environment grew more hostile. All the kingdoms dotted across this land began to collapse, as if the heavens were reaching down to pluck away all the wealth and glory of before.

The Black Desert was one of the first places to be abandoned by the gods. By the Jin dynasty, all civilization here had come to an end, and to this day, an atmosphere of death hangs heavy over this place.

Clutching the notebook left by the British explorer, Julie discussed our route with Asat Amat as we traveled. The book had a record of a cluster of stone graves, not far from the Western Night City, that the expedition had stumbled upon and carefully marked so they could come back to them later.

Although Julie's notebook didn't pinpoint a location, Asat Amat was able to judge from the elevation and position roughly where we needed to be.

That first night, Asat Amat found us a slightly raised bit of land on which we could set up camp. We shoveled a barrier to keep flying sand out, settled the camels, and lit a fire on the side of the dune facing away from the wind.

We were all exhausted from the day's walking. Although

the wind hadn't been too strong, it never let up, a constant annoying presence buffeting us every step of the way. Asat Amat nagged again that this was sandstorm season, and every other day in the Black Desert would throw up weather like this. During the rest of the year, though, the sun was so fierce it drained every drop of moisture from your body.

"That's okay, sweating is a good way to lose weight," Kai joked. "And I could do with a bit of a tan. But this wind sucks. We can't even talk as we're walking—the words get blown right out of our mouths. I'm so bored."

Asat Amat said we were only on the fringes of the Black Desert, and it would be another five days before we got into its heart. Although this was his first trip, he had many friends who'd been here before—and only barely survived.

The terrifying thing about the Black Desert, Asat Amat told us, wasn't getting caught in quicksand or overtaken by golden ants who'd strip a car bare, never mind a human body, and it wasn't the black sandstorms either. According to legend, there was a valley of illusion deep within the desert, and as soon as you stepped in it, you'd see lakes, flowing water, beautiful women, mythological creatures, snow-capped mountains, and lush green fields. Parched and weary, you'd naturally rush to-ward that gorgeous sight, only you'd keep going until you died of thirst and exhaustion, not getting one step closer. This was a demon's trap, luring the unwary to their deaths. But Asat Amat was sure Old Hu would keep us safe from it.

"That might just be a regular mirage," said Julie. "People who don't understand that phenomenon might mistake it for something more sinister."

Little Ye had crept up behind Julie and now tugged her

sleeve and whispered something. Julie turned to the rest of us. "We're just going to look at something on the other side of that dune," she announced.

I thought LittleYe might have needed to relieve herself and been too scared to go off on her own in the dark. She was a nervous little thing. "Make sure you have your flashlights and whistles on you," I said. "And call for help if you need it. Go quickly."

Julie nodded and the pair went off hand in hand, disappearing behind a nearby sand dune. Kai turned to me and asked if he could have more water. I gave him some, knowing that if we didn't find another water source in five or six days, we'd need to start rationing.

I told him as much, a little to frighten him. Even if we failed to find one of the underground rivers, I knew a way of making sure everyone stayed hydrated. It was a method my grandfather had learned in the army—using the sun's heat to evaporate any impure water we managed to find by digging close to the surface, then collecting the condensation, which ought to be drinkable. It would be a cumbersome process, but would serve as a last resort. I'd mentioned it to Asat Amat, who agreed.

The wind increased, and at the same time a couple of piercing whistles came from the other side of the dune. Startled, we all grabbed whatever was closest to hand—shovels, rifles—and rushed over.

Behind the dune, we saw LittleYe, half her body mired in the ground. She struggled as Julie held her arms tight, trying to pull her free. In the confusion, I'm not sure whose voice I heard crying out "Quicksand!"

Aiming our feet for her footprints to prevent being sucked under, we sprinted to her. There was no time to find a rope, so several of us took off our belts, and soon they were looped around her arms. It took surprisingly little effort to yank her free. Back on her feet, Little Ye leaned against Julie, sobbing.

"As soon as we got behind the dune, Little Ye's feet slipped out from under her and her legs disappeared under the sand," Julie explained. "I grabbed hold of her and blew my whistle. It doesn't look like quicksand, or she'd have been sucked under much faster, and I wouldn't have been able to hold on to her on my own. I think there was something firm beneath her feet."

Wiping away her tears, Little Ye nodded. "I felt something under the sand," she told us. "Maybe a stone slab. It gave way under my feet, and I fell."

"Could this be a grave?" Julie wondered aloud. "We should have a look."

As we already had some shovels handy, we were able to dig down right where Little Ye had been standing. Not far beneath the surface, maybe the height of a dune, was a slanting stone wall in which a huge hole had been blasted, probably quite recently. The wind had blown a thin layer of sand over the gap, and as soon as Little Ye stepped onto the spot, she sank into it.

We gaped at the sight and exchanged questioning glances. It was obviously a stone tomb.

How had a regular grave robber found this place in the vastness of the desert? There was absolutely nothing in the surrounding landscape to mark the spot. Could it be that someone else in the world had the ability to read feng shui in the stars, for all I knew even better than my half-baked attempts?

I looked carefully at the shattered stone around the opening.

I'd heard a lot about explosives from my grandfather, who had been in the artillery during his brief army stint. Whoever had pulled off this blast had done a finely calibrated job—only the exterior stone wall was damaged, and the debris directed outward, so nothing inside the tomb would have been damaged.

As we cleared away the sand, a wedge-shaped stone wall was revealed. Apart from the side that had been blown open, the rest remained buried beneath the desert's surface.

It was a typical tomb from the Wei-Jin period: enormous slabs of mountain rock shaped into arches, the cracks sealed with fish glue. Structures like this were a common sight around the Western Night City. And now these tombs had been completely covered by the desert, making them nearly impossible to find. Professor Chen conjectured that the strong winds from the last few days had been responsible for exposing part of this one, though unfortunately, grave robbers had been faster to get here than our archaeological team.

The space beyond the hole was pitch-dark. A few of us went in, flashlights at the ready, and found ourselves in a vault about the size of a small apartment, with four or five coffins scattered around it. They'd all been pried open and flung aside, leaving a mess everywhere.

These coffins were all different sizes, as if belonging to a mass grave. The only corpse left was a young girl's, her hair long and worn in many braids. Her head was reasonably well preserved, but her body was broken and crumbling. The inhabitants of the other coffins were gone, probably taken by the thieves.

That's how it is with Xinjiang graves. Just as valuable as the treasures are the dried-out corpses. I'd heard Professor Chen list the types of ancient remains: wet corpses, which retained moisture in their bodies; waxed corpses, specially treated for preservation; frozen corpses, found in arctic regions where snow remained on the ground year-round; cured corpses, which ended up similar to zombies; and other varieties, such as stuffed corpses, like medical specimens.

Even dried corpses came in different sorts: those made by having drying agents such as lime or charcoal placed in the coffin with them, and those made by mummifying techniques like the ones used in ancient Egypt.

The desiccated corpses of Xinjiang, however, were formed naturally, a product of the hot, dry, sterile environment. Once they were past a certain age, such corpses became quite valuable, with overseas museums and collectors willing to pay top dollar for them.

Seeing the tomb so badly vandalized and the other corpses gone, the professor could only sigh in disappointment. He told his students to restore the place as best they could and see if there was anything worth salvaging.

Worried that he might be too agitated, I suggested that the professor take a rest. Before allowing Kai to lead him back to the campsite, he gave Hao Aiguo some final instructions about being sure to record every detail of the layout of the tomb.

The next day, the wind continued gusting at a steady speed. As we set off, the professor came to me and confided that the tomb couldn't have been broken into more than three or four days ago, and a team of robbers might well be just ahead of us in the Black Desert. We had to catch up with them without delay, he urged.

I muttered something in agreement, making a mental note

to stay well clear of these other robbers. Anyone in the same line of work is a rival, and if these guys were prepared enough to blast through stone walls with military-grade explosives, they probably had other weapons up their sleeves. I was certainly not eager to encounter them. Not for my own sake, but I was now responsible for these archaeologists, none of whom looked like they'd be any good in a fight.

Then again, it wouldn't be that easy for two groups of people to run into each other in the vast desert, even if we'd wanted to. If the sand dune hadn't happened to be the highest point near us at dusk yesterday, we wouldn't have set up camp there and wouldn't have stumbled upon this tomb. Could such a coincidence happen again? Besides, for all we knew, these robbers had taken their dried corpses and gone back home.

CHAPTER TEN

FOR THE NEXT TEN DAYS, WE WANDERED DEEPER AND DEEPER INTO the Black Desert. Finally, we lost track of the underground Zidu River, and for several days found ourselves going in circles. In the ancient local language, "zidu" means "shadow," and this river really was like a shadow, impossible to catch hold of. Asat Amat's eyes were bloodshot, and finally, even he threw up his hands in defeat. There was no help for it—it seemed Old Hu didn't want us to go beyond this point.

We were all dog-tired, unable to walk a step farther. There hadn't been any wind for days now, and the sun seemed to hang in the sky much longer than was warranted. To save water, we each dug trenches in the ground during the day, climbing in and covering ourselves with sailcloth, hoping the deeper, cooler layers of sand would help preserve the moisture in our bodies. We only traveled at night and in the early morning, half the time on our camels, half the time on foot.

Now, though, we would surely run out of rations and water if we kept moving forward. If we delayed any more than a day or two, we'd end up having to slaughter the camels for food on the return journey.

Looking at this group of people, their bodies bone weary and their lips cracking from dehydration, I knew most of them had reached their limits. The sun was getting high in the sky, and temperatures were climbing. I gave the signal for them to start digging trenches.

After everyone was settled, Julie came over to me and Asat Amat, brandishing a section in the British explorer's notebook. "Look, he also lost the path of the Zidu River once he got too far into the Black Desert. He writes about a sea of death, with not even a single blade of grass to be seen. Then he comes upon two black hills of magnetic rock, facing each other in the second sun, like a pair of ancient warriors in black armor, silently guarding a secret from the dawn of time. Passing through this valley, like a gate, he saw the city appear before him."

"Magnetic hills?" I said. My watch had been stopping constantly for the last two days, or else suddenly getting faster or slower. I'd presumed this was because it was cheap and not up to desert conditions, but what if we were actually in the vicinity of these hills?

Asat Amat thought he remembered a story like that about the Black Desert, only in his version it was the Zaklaman Mountains, one red and one white, the burial sites of ancient gods.

Julie went on, "If these hills really do exist, then the Zidu might be forced to flow deeper underground by the magnetic field, which is why we can't find it. I think we should stop trying to locate the river. If this British explorer is right, the hills aren't far from us. Mr. Hu, I'll need you to use your astrological feng shui tonight. Don't forget what we agreed—if we make it to the Jingjue City, I'm doubling your fee."

I'd never thought we had much chance of reaching Jingjue City, but now it seemed I had no choice. I'd give it a go that night, and if we found the Zaklaman Mountains, my fee would increase to twenty thousand American dollars. If I failed, we'd have to head home.

To be honest, I couldn't have said whether I even wanted to find Jingjue City. After hearing the story of the Jingjue queen, a mysterious, seductive image flitted into my brain and wouldn't get out. It felt like a shapeless force was calling me across the desert. I had no idea whether Julie and the professor felt it too, not to mention those explorers who set off across the sands and never returned.

That day felt unnaturally long. If I could, I would have taken my rifle and shot the sun out of the sky. We dug our sand pits as deep as we could but never found any cooler ground.

Even deep in our trenches beneath thick canvas, we felt like we were trapped in blazing ovens. Fragile Little Ye seemed to suffer some kind of sun damage and began babbling in her sleep.

Worried she was ill, we touched her forehead, but it was just as hot as the sand around her, so we couldn't tell if she had a fever. No matter how hard we shook her, she wouldn't wake up.

We still had enough water for five days, plus a couple of pouches full of fermented milk as a backup. No use hanging on to it. I grabbed one of the pouches and got Julie to feed her a few mouthfuls, then followed that up with some pills.

The medicine calmed her down, but she didn't regain consciousness. She was probably suffering from severe dehydration, which meant trouble. I explained the situation to the professor.

We had two choices. We could turn around and head back, which would mean slaughtering and eating our camels in the last few days of our retreat, drinking brackish water extracted from the sand, and walking once all the camels were gone. Even so, that wouldn't ensure Little Ye's survival. The alternative was to stick to our guns and continue the search for Jingjue City. If we reached it and there was a water source there, Little Ye's life might be saved.

Professor Chen pondered the matter. Our situation was dire, and even though archaeologists are meant to have a spirit of self-sacrifice, Little Ye was so young that we needed to think of our responsibility toward her. The first plan was more certain, but without sufficient water, the road back would be very difficult; the second option was riskier, but we were close to Zaklaman, with at least a sixty percent chance of reaching Jingjue—though while the ancient city had definitely been built over water sources, who knew whether those had since dried up. He asked everyone for their opinion on what to do next.

Kai went first. "Look how much my waistline's shrunk! I say we don't pause for a second, but as soon as the sun sets, we turn around and go back. That way we might actually stay alive."

Hao Aiguo and Sa Dipeng agreed with him, though in a more somber manner.

In the end, there were slightly more of us who thought it was worth taking a chance and forging ahead. We'd already sacrificed so much to get here, it seemed like a shame to give up now. Besides, if there was water at Jingjue, Little Ye's life would be saved, and we wouldn't have to drink gritty underground water on the way back, which even the healthy people would find hard. Given Little Ye's condition, trying to bring her back now would amount to a death sentence.

That was the viewpoint of Julie, Chu Jian, the professor, and me. Apart from the unconscious Little Ye, only old Asat Amat hadn't expressed an opinion. Everyone looked at him. If he voted to turn back, that would make it four against four— but as our guide, his opinion would carry more weight.

"Sir, please think before you speak," I said to him. "This concerns Little Ye's life. What should we do?"

Sucking on his long pipe, Asat Amat screwed up his eyes and glared at the sun before speaking. "Naturally, I'm going along with Old Hu. Just like there's only one sun in the sky, ah, the world only has one true god. He'll lead us."

I pointed at the sky. "Then hurry up and ask the old guy what we should do."

Asat Amat tapped his pipe and slipped it back into his belt, then pulled out his tattered prayer mat and sincerely prepared for his devotions, palms facing him as he recited his verses, his expression solemn and humble, the usual cunning momentarily absent.

We couldn't make out what exactly he was chanting.

Growing impatient, Kai cried out, "Old man, aren't you done yet?"

Asat Amat's eyes blinked open, and he smiled. "Old Hu will show us the way," he said. As he spoke, he pulled out a five-cent coin and showed it to everyone. This was his augury: heads we continued, tails we turned back. He invited Professor Chen to toss it into the air.

We looked at each other, uncertain whether to laugh or cry. The professor flipped the coin high in the air, and we all looked up to see it glitter in the sun, then plummet down to land perfectly upright, wedged in the sand.

This was a one-in-a-million chance. Asat Amat shook his head again and again, despair filling his face. He'd forgotten we were in the Black Desert, a place abandoned by Old Hu, and therefore couldn't look to him for direction.

As we were scratching our heads at this mystery, Julie suddenly exclaimed, "Hang on, isn't that Zaklaman over there?"

In the empty vastness of the desert, your view is unobstructed for hundreds of miles. Looking where Julie was pointing, past the coin and all the way to the horizon, we saw a faint black line, too distant to say what it was.

We hurriedly pulled out our binoculars and focused on what turned out to be a dark mountain ridge, lying like a black dragon across the desert sands. There was a gap right in its center—a mountain pass, exactly where the British explorer's notebook had said it would be.

A year ago, Julie's father had led an expedition to find Jingjue City, using these same clues. Had they seen this mystic mountain too? If they made it all the way there, what did they find? What could have prevented them from returning?

These thoughts sent a shiver through me, despite the blazing heat, but the fears were quickly doused by a rush of excitement. We'd risked everything on this long journey, and here at long last was the entrance to the ancient kingdom of Jingjue.

On the other hand, Asat Amat had warned that the Black Desert was a place of illusions, where mirages frequently lured people to their deaths. Could it be that these mountains weren't real?

Running the possibilities through my mind, I decided it was unlikely. Desert mirages were caused by the bending of light, and they usually presented scenarios that couldn't exist in this environment. More than one person had mentioned this black mountain ridge, so it was likely to be the real thing.

Seeing as Jingjue City wasn't too far away, as soon as darkness fell, we'd be able to set out toward it. We didn't have much information to go on, and most of what we did have was conjecture and legend. The only reliable piece of evidence was a blurry black-and-white photograph, which didn't help much. Whether we'd be able to find this place, or if it even existed, was still uncertain.

Still, as soon as the sun began to dip, we set off for the Zaklaman Mountains. Fixing our eyes on the target, we trotted along for more than half the night before reaching the mountain pass. The moonlight poured down like water, making the desert look like a vast ocean, and rising from that sea of sand was the twin black masses of the Zaklaman, an arresting sight.

We'd called them mountains, but it seemed more accurate to say they were two enormous slabs of black stone. At their highest points, they were dozens of miles tall, leaving a trail of shorter hills, a spine running down into the sand, most of it lying beneath the surface. Underground was also where these two huge bodies were joined. This pass was just a small crack in a gigantic piece of rock.

The black rock contained magnetic elements. Not overwhelmingly strong, but enough to affect our instruments, and as we started to climb, we felt all the metallic items we were carrying slowly grow heavier.

The dark stone didn't reflect any of the moon's light, leaving the mountain pass pitch-dark. Apart from the unconscious Little Ye, we all scrambled down from our camels. I reminded everyone to keep their eyes open wide. We were traveling into the demon's mouth and needed to be on our guard.

Asat Amat and I led the way, with Kai and Chu Jian bringing up the rear. Julie and the others formed a column in the middle, making sure Little Ye was all right. We slowly made our way into the valley.

In ancient times, people called this place a spirit hill. Legend had it that two sages were buried here. That was probably just myth, but from the feng shui point of view, this was a very strong position, conquering everything around it, the black mountain ridge dominating the landscape. It would hardly be surprising if it turned out the Jingjue queen lay behind this powerful edifice.

After the moon crossed the center of the sky, the canyon, which ran north-south, grew even more inky black. We felt our way forward, growing more and more uneasy, beginning to doubt that the fabled Jingjue City really stood on the other side, our fears for Little Ye's condition growing. We'd been treating her dehydration with large quantities of salted water, but if we didn't find a water source within three days, she was doomed.

Our watches had all stopped working long ago, making it impossible to say how long we'd been walking. My instincts told me the sun would rise soon. The camels' breathing was growing ragged, and something seemed to be unsettling them.

Asat Amat blew his whistle and cooed at them, trying every trick he knew to calm his herd down. These were all strapping males, chosen for their resilience, and even after so many days in the desert, this was the first time we'd seen them in such distress.

These alarming noises in the already-terrifying darkness filled our hearts with terror. Julie worried that Little Ye would be flung from her perch and asked Hao Aiguo to help carry her instead.

I called Kai over and told him to do his bit and give Little Ye a piggyback ride. This valley felt like a place we shouldn't linger in, and we needed to get through it as quickly as possible. Kai certainly didn't object to having a pretty girl on his back, and it was no hardship to him at all, given how thin she was.

We tried to hurry ahead, but no matter how Asat Amat urged them, the camels simply refused to take one more step. Asat Amat began to suspect demons at work, then changed his mind and said it must be Old Hu himself blocking our way and we should turn back immediately.

The end of the valley was not far off, and we'd surely have faced a revolt if we told the group to turn around. Julie said to me, "Maybe there really is something up ahead spooking the camels. Let's shed some light on the matter before making any decisions."

That made sense. I pulled out a flare, activated it, and flung it directly in front of us so it illuminated the next little stretch of the valley. Nothing unexpected—dull black stone on either side, yellow sand beneath our feet.

Walking forward, I threw a second flare. In its gleam, I saw a figure in the distance. Hurrying over, we found someone in white robes, a cloth wrapped around his head, a bundle on his back. He sat on the ground, unmoving. It was a corpse.

CHAPTER ELEVEN

WE WERE ALL STUNNED. THERE WAS NOTHING STRANGE ABOUT EN-
countering dead people in the desert, but something about
this body was different. His face was covered, except for his
eyes, which were open wide and glaring up at the sky.

He had died recently, maybe just a few days ago. His exposed skin was only a little dried out, but the strange thing was
that it had a green tinge to it, though the lingering light of the
flare tinted it blue.

Several people wanted to go over to him, but I held them
back. It wasn't clear how he'd died, and until we knew that, it
might be dangerous to get too close. Then Chu Jian shouted,
"Look, another one!"

My scalp tingled. Two corpses so close to each other.

Could there be more? I flung out a few more flares, illuminating our surroundings, and sure enough, there were a total of four bodies, some upright and some on the ground, all dressed alike and all with wide-open eyes, as if in fear. Scattered on the ground were a few AK-47s and rucksacks.

I pulled out my shovel in case I needed to defend myself, and went over to inspect each item. The guns were loaded. I knew Xinjiang poachers sometimes used foreign-made Remingtons or Type 56 assault rifles, but Russian-manufactured AK-47s? Could these be the grave robbers who'd blown a hole in the stone wall of the tomb?

Nudging open one of the rucksacks, I found it stuffed with military-grade dynamite, covered in Cyrillic words. It was perfectly normal for these bandits to have smuggled explosives. What I didn't understand was how they'd come to die here in the desert, armed to the teeth as they were.

With the barrel of my rifle, I carefully lifted the scarf of the corpse closest to me. His mouth was open wide, as if he'd died screaming. I didn't want to look any closer. No matter what had happened, the most important thing was to leave this valley-grave as quickly as possible. Grabbing the rucksack of explosives, which might come in useful later, I turned to tell everyone to get moving.

Before I could speak, Hao Aiguo was striding over. "It doesn't matter whether or not these people are tomb robbers. We can't leave them out in the open," he said. "Let's bring them with us and bury them beyond the valley." He made his way to the corpse.

This wasn't good. "Get away from him, you idiot!" I snapped. "You don't know—"

But it was too late. All of a sudden, a snake burst out of the corpse's mouth. It was about twelve inches long, covered in glittering scales, with a fleshy black hood around its head. This all happened in a flash, and before we knew it, it had launched itself straight at Hao Aiguo's face.

Hao Aiguo's eyesight was poor, but even if he'd been able to see clearly, there would have been no time to react. In the flickering light of the flare, I made my move out of pure instinct. The shovel in my hand sliced through the air, cutting the snake clean in half.

Shaken, Aiguo sat down hard on the ground, his whole body trembling. He managed to smile. "That was close. I almost—"

Before he could finish his sentence, the severed snake head began thrashing, and like an arrow from a bow, it shot up and bit Hao Aiguo in the neck. Having thought the bisected snake was dead, I'd let down my guard. Once again, my shovel sprang up, but too late this time.

Hao Aiguo's face froze, and a gurgling sound came from his throat. He was trying to speak, but already his skin was turning dull green. Then he stopped moving altogether, sitting very still where he was. I went a little closer. He was dead.

All this happened in an instant. The professor fainted to the ground. Before I even had time to feel sorrow or shock for Aiguo's passing, something cool touched the side of my neck. Turning my head, I saw that a similar snake had climbed up to my shoulder without my noticing and was sticking out its forked tongue, the coiled muscle of its body tensing back, ready to strike. At this range, and knowing how quickly these creatures moved, I couldn't avoid it.

In our whole group, only Kai was a good shot, and right now his arms were carrying Little Ye rather than a gun. A basin of cold water seemed to splash over my heart. I was going to die this very minute, not even living long enough to see the sun rise.

As the snake reared up, I knew I was doomed. Soon its head would dart forward, and its teeth would pump its prey— me—full of venom. My neck and face were completely exposed, with nowhere to hide. There was nothing I could do.

Just as I was closing my eyes and preparing to meet my fate, I heard a loud click and saw a blinding flash of light. The inky gloom of the canyon was suddenly lit up as bright as day, and the snake, already halfway to my neck, was so dazzled by this unexpected brilliance that it slipped from my shoulder.

This can't have taken more than a second. Before the snake hit the ground, I was already swinging my shovel, smashing its head flat. A viscous black fluid oozed from its skull, and I quickly jumped back to avoid getting it on my feet. I knew how lucky I was. By the looks of it, this venom acted swiftly, spreading lethally through your bloodstream within an instant of being bitten.

Looking up for the source of the miraculous light, I saw Julie's camera. It was always by her side—she'd been documenting our entire journey, step by step. I'd never thought it would save my life, but her quick reaction managed to prevent my death. Otherwise I'd now be off to see Old Hu.

There was no time to thank her, though. For all we knew, this valley could be a giant nest of these snakes. Waving urgently, I signaled to everyone to get moving. Anything that needed to be said could wait till we were out of this accursed place.

The camels seemed to sense that the immediate threat was gone and were calmer than before. Chu Jian and the rest picked up Hao Aiguo's body, as well as the unconscious Little Ye and Professor Chen, and loaded them all onto our mounts.

Asat Amat whistled to lead the camels forward, and by the dim light of the remaining flares and flashlights, we made our way out of the Zaklaman valley as quickly as humanly possible.

We didn't stop moving until we'd reached the open land at the end of the passageway. Now we could finally lay Hao Aiguo to rest. The sun hadn't risen yet, and the moon and stars were nowhere to be seen. They say it's darkest before the dawn. Aiguo's face was frozen in a rictus of fear, his eyes wide behind his glasses. Beneath our flashlights, his greenish skin looked peculiar, adding to the tragedy of the moment.

A cold wind gusted through the valley, hitting us hard and jolting the professor awake. Remembering what had happened, he struggled over to Aiguo's corpse and flung himself on it, weeping too hard to speak. I helped him up and tried to say something comforting, but the words died in my mouth.

I'd known Hao Aiguo for almost a month, and had come to enjoy jokingly calling him "that old fossil." I appreciated his fast-talking, quick-thinking personality, and now, all of a sudden I couldn't even deal with my own grief.

The others were quietly shedding tears. All of a sudden, a fissure appeared in the sky, something dark and red pouring from it. The sun was finally showing itself. Our heads turned in unison, and we stared at the east.

The light slowly turned the color of roses, then blood, before shattering into a million gilded beams. The arc of the sun appeared, and in that instant, the endless desert melted into pure gold, straight from the imperial furnaces.

And there it was, set in this gleaming expanse: a magnificent city displaying itself before us. Countless broken walls and fallen ramparts, buildings of wood and brick, and numerous towers rising into the air, the most prominent of which was of black stone, now tilting to one side, quietly slumping in the very center of the citadel.

Every detail of this was exactly the same as in Julie's black-and-white photograph. Even after two thousand years, the ruins of Jingjue City remained where they'd always been, in the deepest reaches of the desert.

Back in the day, Jingjue had been home to between fifty and sixty thousand people. Other ancient kingdoms, such as Kroraina, even at their height, never supported more than twenty thousand, plus an army of three thousand or so.

The city was in poor repair now. After its millennia-long abandonment, it was hard to tell whether some portions were sand dunes or battlements, and most of its towers were weathered, if not fallen. Even so, it was still possible to imagine what a splendid sight this must have been in its heyday.

His arm around Hao Aiguo's shoulders, the professor pointed shakily at Jingjue City. "Look, over there," he said in a hoarse voice. "Haven't you always wanted to see that mystic place? Open your eyes; it's just ahead. We've reached it at last."

I felt something twist inside me. Had the old man lost his mind from sadness? Walking over quickly, I pulled him away from the corpse. "Professor, Hao Aiguo has left us," I said softly. "Let him rest in peace. It's a shame he didn't make it to Jingjue—you'll have to complete our mission for his sake. Please, sir, pull yourself together."

Julie and the students came over to comfort him too, and I handed the professor over to them. Turning to Julie, my heart full of gratitude, I said, "You saved my life. I won't say thank you; just consider that I now owe you a life in return. Oh, and a deal is a deal. Jingjue's up ahead, so that's twenty thousand American dollars I'm due."

At the mention of money, Kai hurried over. "That's twenty thousand each, forty thousand all together," he specified breathlessly. "In cash, please."

Julie rolled her eyes at us. "Take it easy, both of you," she said through clenched teeth. "I'll be sure to get all the money to you as soon as we get home, not one penny less."

It hit me that I'd been tactless to mention money at that moment, but my mind was jumbled after recent events, and the words just popped out of my mouth. Trying to pull the conversation around, I stammered the only thing I could think to say: "This . . . city . . . It's quite big. . . ."

Julie glared at me. "Over the last few days, I've seen that the two of you are extraordinarily talented, with an impressive amount of experience," she said. "I never expected you to be so mercenary. I guess my first impression was wrong. I only have one piece of advice for you both: remember, there are things in this world even more valuable than cash."

I had nothing to say to that. But Kai did. "My dear Miss Yang, you live beneath the Stars and Stripes in the United States of America. Your father was some Wall Street big shot, and I'm guessing you've never gone hungry. You've never had to worry where your next meal was coming from. So you don't understand anything about our lives, the circumstances we grew up in, and you don't have the right to judge us. And don't bother telling us how to live. Poor people don't live, we only survive. If you don't like what I'm saying, just pretend you didn't hear. We've brought you to Jingjue City, as per our contract, and now we're awaiting further instructions."

Kai had started out his speech all puffed up with righteous indignation, but by the last sentence he seemed to have remembered that Julie was our employer and abruptly switched to a more servile tone.

I found my voice. "Julie, about Mr. Hao . . . I did my best. I'm really sorry that wasn't enough."

Julie nodded at me, ignored Kai altogether, and got out her water bottle to hydrate the professor and Little Ye. Professor Chen still looked shaken by Aiguo's death, but a drink seemed to bring him back to himself. We discussed the matter quickly and decided to bury Hao Aiguo in the sand near the entrance to the valley. He'd spent his life studying the culture of the Western Regions, and would probably have wanted to remain here, occupying this mysterious city in the desert for all eternity.

After digging a pit in the sand, we wrapped his body in a blanket and lowered him in. Once we'd covered the grave, I stuck a shovel in front of it. That was all we could provide by way of a tombstone.

Eight of us left now. We stood in silence by Hao Aiguo's grave for a long time before we felt ready to move on.

Having dealt with the deceased, we had to do what we could for the living, which meant finding a water source as quickly as possible; otherwise it wouldn't be long before Little Ye was buried in the sand too.

We began gathering our possessions, getting ready to enter the city. Now that we were finally at our destination, I hoped there wouldn't be any more trouble. If we lost anyone else, I didn't think I'd be able to bring myself to accept my fee for this job.

Julie was trembling slightly, though I couldn't tell whether out of fear, anxiety, or excitement. She pulled out a crucifix and said a prayer in a low voice, then turned to us and said, "Let's go."

Unexpectedly, it was Asat Amat who now dragged his heels. He shook his head violently like a baby's rattle, refusing to set foot in the Jingjue ruins. He said Hao Aiguo's death was a bad omen, and the poisonous snake was a demon's familiar.

There was no convincing him, so we decided Asat Amat could set up camp at the foot of the Zaklaman Mountains, where he'd watch over the camels and wait for our return.

I thought of telling Kai to stay too, to keep an eye on Asat Amat in case he thought of running off. We needed him—and needed the camels even more. It was hard to imagine how long it would take us to get home on foot without them. But then I thought Asat Amat had stayed with us this long and still hadn't received a cent for his work, so he'd probably stick around. After all, he'd been promised a generous amount of money, enough to support him for the rest of his life.

Still, I'd been cheated enough times to know it was best to take precautions. Pulling Asat Amat to one side, I asked him, "So tell me, how does Old Hu punish liars and traitors?"

"Oh, their home and money turn to sand. And all the salt

in their food turns to sand, ah, so they starve to death. Like dying in the Black Desert. Afterward, they end up in a part of hell that's full of hot sand, where one thousand eight hundred types of punishment wait for them."

He seemed sincere, so I relaxed. His religious beliefs would keep him honest.

CHAPTER TWELVE

SEVEN OF US ENTERED THE ANCIENT CITY, WITH CHU JIAN CARRYING the unconscious Little Ye on his back. The rest of us had to carry all our equipment and weaponry between us, not to mention food and water supplies. It was a considerable burden.

I remember my grandfather telling me an old army saying: you can tell a soldier by the extra forty pounds—meaning the minimum weight of a regular soldier's battle pack is forty pounds. Those chosen to carry machine guns or wear antitank armor had to shoulder even more.

Kai and I were used to carrying heavy loads, but Professor Chen and the other eggheads were clearly struggling.

It wasn't far from the mountain pass to the ruins, and we only had to stop for one meal before reaching the gates. The walls around here were full of cracks, and the moat was filled with sand, so there was nothing to stop us from walking right in. And now we were in the ancient city itself, the ruins around us filled with a deathly silence.

It was nothing at all like I'd imagined, and I couldn't help being disappointed. The streets and buildings had all collapsed, or at least were badly damaged. What looked like a magnificent city from a distance turned out, close up, to be nothing but rotting wood and crumbling stone poking out of the sand. What treasure could possibly be in a place like this?

Only in the vast wooden beams could you still see a trace of the former splendor, even though they too were falling apart and most of the scarlet paint had long since peeled off them.

We tried to enter some of the houses close to the wall, only to find that even though they appeared sheltered from the desert, every one of them was filled with sand, almost to the roof.

The legend was that the city had been destroyed in the fires of war. The invading army had marched right up to the palace; then, as the battle drew to a close, a black sandstorm swept over Jingjue, burying both its inhabitants and the attackers indiscriminately beneath a deep layer of sand. It wasn't till the nineteenth century that the sand shifted again to reveal the ruins.

Everything we saw was just as the story predicted, apart from the lack of dried-out corpses—but for all we knew, they were buried beneath the sand.

I quickly decided there was nothing here, but Professor Chen and his students seemed fascinated by everything to do with the ancient city. You could probably have sat them in front of any disintegrating wall and they'd have happily stared at it for hours on end.

Before they got too engrossed, I reminded them that Little Ye was still unwell, and we had to make sure we saved her before doing anything else. It looked like sand had filled every crevice here, and we had no hope of finding any wells, so why not go have a look at the palace? That was probably our best bet for finding any drinkable water.

Professor Chen smacked his forehead. "I'm an old scatter-brain. You're right, we should make sure Little Ye is all right. Let's go straight to the palace, then. Every kingdom in the desert was built on top of underground rivers, and sometimes they flowed right through the main buildings. The palace is usually in the center of the city."

We oriented ourselves and made our way toward the center. Kai murmured to me, "Tianyi, do you know what my mouth is watering for right now? I'd love some honey-dew melon, or some of those really plump purple grapes. Or even just a slice of watermelon." He sighed. "All this talk is just making me thirstier. I swear I can feel smoke rising in my throat, it's that dry. If we find this underground river, I'm going to jump right into it and have a long soak."

"The Jingjue queen was known for her fancy lifestyle," I told him. "I'm sure she always had watermelons soaking in the cool underground streams. Of course, any that are left will be fossils by now, and the remaining grapes are surely raisins."

"What kind of place is this?" grumbled Kai. "I can't believe anyone actually wanted to live here. Next time, never mind twenty thousand American dollars. You could offer me a mountain of gold and silver and I still wouldn't set foot in the desert. Of all the ways to die, thirst has to be the worst."

His mention of death reminded me of Hao Aiguo. He hadn't lived long after being bitten by that strange snake, but who knew how much he'd suffered in those few moments? And that snake—its head hooded with a black tumor that turned out to be filled with poisonous liquid, able to leap up and bite even after being cut in half . . . Even Julie hadn't seen anything like it before. Would there be more of those creatures in this place?

The seven of us made our way cautiously along the path, ruined buildings to either side. Where they blocked the road, we had to make our way around them, so it took a long time to reach the center of the city. There, the streets were wider, and although they were still covered in sand, it was easier to tell their layout.

Apart from the leaning black tower, there were no other large buildings around here. Never mind the grand palace, there weren't even any decent-looking houses. All we saw were mud walls, wrecked from years of weathering.

Professor Chen said the palace might have been built underground, to keep out the sand. Our best bet was to climb the tower and look around, hoping to spot the entrance.

The tower looked like it was built of Zaklaman stone. It was six stories high and, apart from the slight tilt, appeared reasonably sturdy. We hadn't seen these building materials used anywhere else in the city. The other odd feature was an olive-shaped black stone topping the structure. The lowest level had several entrance archways, but they were all blocked with sand.

Professor Chen fussily put on his glasses and looked up, then looked again with his binoculars. "That's right—why didn't I think of this before?" he muttered to himself.

Before I could ask him what he had discovered, he'd hunched over and burrowed his way through the main door, as if desperate to check on something. We quickly followed as best we could, clambering over the sand. Fortunately, once we rose past ground level, the way was relatively clear.

The walls of the tower were covered in densely carved words in some mysterious language, and a black stone statue stood at the center of each level. On the first floor was a perfectly ordinary goat, while the second had a kneeling human figure, more or less life-size, with a high nose and sunken eyes. On the third level, we were startled to see the twin of the statue we'd encountered in the little town where we'd taken shelter from the sandstorm, with the same enormous eyes.

Professor Chen was jubilant. "So I guessed right! The big-eyed statues that have appeared all around here originate from the Jingjue Kingdom. And they must all be made of black stone from the Zaklaman Mountains."

"Professor, what's this tower for?" Sa Dipeng asked. "Why is there a statue on every floor?"

"My theory is that this tower was used to represent the city's different inhabitants. The first floor, with its goat statue, stands for domesticated animals, and if my guess is right, there should be an underground level below it for the hungry ghosts stuck in hell. The second story is for regular people, most of them Muslims and slaves from the Western Regions. Then this large-eyed creature whose stone oval right on top is the shape of an eye. My guess is that this place is also a totem showing how important seeing is to this culture. Let's hurry and see what's above us—what the upper levels of the Jingjue world look like."

Kai butted in. "Even a dummy like me can figure that one out," he boasted. "I bet you the next stage has to be the queen herself." With that, he rushed up to the next floor. I followed closely behind.

The sight that awaited us was completely unexpected. The statue on the next level had the body of a serpent with a human head, plus four sturdy limbs, the back two belonging to some wild animal, the front two like human arms, one hand holding a sword and the other a shield. The face was a man's, ferocious, with staring eyes, like some kind of sentinel, with a fleshy black hood around his head, just like the monstrous snakes we had encountered in the desert.

One by one, the professor and the others huffed their way up the stairs. They were all stunned by the bizarre statue. They muttered among themselves about how it might be the guardian spirit of the kingdom, and how the black oval on its head was the same shape as the one on top of the tower, maybe showing that the Jingjue people really did think the eyes were the source of all power. If this deity was below the queen, that must mean she really was regarded as a goddess. We hurried up to the fifth floor to see.

Before we got there, though, the morning breeze gusting through the tower seemed to revive Little Ye, and her eyes suddenly opened. Julie quickly knelt beside her, feeding her a little water from her bottle. Little Ye was still weak and badly dehydrated, but now that she had regained consciousness, we could treat her with large quantities of cold salted water over the next day or two. She would get back to full health.

Still eager to know what other mysterious objects were waiting for us in the tower, not to mention hoping to find the location of the palace entrance, we carefully helped Little Ye up to the fifth level.

As we trudged up the stairs, all kinds of possibilities flitted through my mind—every combination of humans and beasts—except the one that confronted us: nothing at all. The fifth floor was completely empty, without even a plinth to show where a statue might have been. The only difference was that the mysterious writing on the walls was denser than below.

"Could the statue have been destroyed?" I asked Professor Chen. "Or taken by looters?"

The professor considered the matter. "That's hard to say. Let's look at the top floor to see if that sheds any light."

Filled with curiosity, we made our way up to the final level. Here we found a massive black throne, on which had been placed the statue of a woman dressed in fine robes. A veil covered her face, obscuring her features. Even so, it was clear that this was the Jingjue queen, exactly as represented on the wall paintings in the ancient tombs.

Immediately, the students began squabbling, guessing what her face must have looked like.

I didn't understand. "What's the deal with this lady?" I asked. "Why not let anyone see her face?"

Kai snickered. "My guess is false advertising. She claims

to be the great beauty of the Western Regions, but I bet she's some freak show under that veil. Otherwise, what's she got to hide? Still, I've got to say that her figure isn't bad."

"You're a pig," Julie snapped in disgust. "Imagine saying that about any woman, let alone one who's been dead two thousand years!"

"That's right," I chimed in. "Besides, everything we've seen in the city is exactly like in the legends. For all we know, the queen really is a demon, and if you say one more word this statue might come to life and bite you in the throat. But enough wild guesses. Let's hear what our professor has to say."

Professor Chen had been silent ever since we reached the sixth floor, as if pulling together the various clues in his head. He seemed to have reached a conclusion and, seeing us all look at him inquiringly, obligingly explained: "Just as I said earlier, this tower is probably a representation of this society's spiritual beliefs, with a clear gradation of status from lowest to highest, from least to most noble. The Jingjue Kingdom is made up of descendants of the Guidong tribe, a people who've been completely wiped out and who haven't left a single artifact behind. We have no information about their origins or ancestry. Our greatest discovery so far has been this totem of the eye, which will definitely be an enormous breakthrough in the study of the Western Regions. With this as proof, many riddles that have been puzzling scholars for years will finally be solved."

"But why was the fifth floor empty?" asked Kai.

Suddenly, I remembered Julie's words as we stood in the Gumo prince's tomb, and blurted out, "An empty space—like a parallel dimension!"

Professor Chen nodded. "That's exactly right. Above the

guardian spirit is an indescribable space, and only after that do we come to the queen, as if to indicate that she controls the space of unknowing. And above her is that great black eye, to show that the queen's powers stem from her eyes."

This sent a shiver through all of us. Could it possibly be that this world contained something that lay beyond human comprehension, a space that none of us could ever hope to understand? If the queen could control this strange realm with her eyes alone, then she really must be some sort of demon. Fortunately, she was safely dead.

Seeing how worried we were, Professor Chen quickly added, "Don't be scared. Ancient rulers often used these kinds of myths to control their peasants, as well as to strengthen their own positions. Look at all the emperors in the Central Plains who claimed to be dragons in human form, descended directly from heaven. In the end, weren't those all legends made up to fool the commoners? It's not at all surprising that this queen would make a big deal of never showing her face, creating all kinds of rumors and stories around herself. When I talk about the significance of this tower, I mean its archaeological importance. All this information will be invaluable to academics."

As the tower contained nothing but these statues, the only thing left for us to do was to go out onto the balcony and survey the ruins. From up here, even with the sand blurring the outlines of the city, it was clear that the ruins lay in the shape of an eye.

Staring down at Jingjue, Professor Chen said to me, "Comrade Hu, your knowledge of feng shui is unparalleled. What do you think of this layout?"

I silently cursed the old man for quizzing me at a time like this, when our first priority ought to be finding the palace and its water source. Or did he believe the queen's tomb also lay underground? I began studying the geography carefully.

Pointing at the Zaklaman Mountains to the north, I said, "Professor, look. That black mountain range resembles a dark dragon slinking through the sand, or it would, if not for the mountain pass cutting it in two, turning it into a couple of snakes. My uninformed guess is that the gap is man-made, and the stone that used to fill it was taken to make this tower and all the statues we saw. After all, every ancient emperor began preparing his grave almost as soon as he seized power. If there really is an underground river beneath this city, then it should be an echo of the Zaklaman, following the same path. The Jingjue queen must have been an intelligent, determined woman. She knew black dragons were unlucky, so she got her subjects to cleave this one in two, nailing it in place and forcing it to guard her tomb for all eternity. And so this city has become a treasure trove. If her grave really is right in the center, then it must be huge. That's what I don't understand, sir. I'm sure she's buried beneath the ground, but you say her palace is there too. Would there really be room for both?"

The professor smiled. "I knew you wouldn't let me down. That's exactly right. I think her tomb and palace are both underground, but not squashed together. Rather, there are likely three levels: a fortress up top, the palace below that, and then, right at the bottom, her eternal resting place. The Jingjue Kingdom was powerful enough to enslave hundreds of thousands from neighboring lands. If they had enough manpower to carve a hole through the Zaklaman Mountain range, surely it wouldn't have been too much of a problem to create a massive underground complex too."

There were rumors that more than one team of explorers had found their way into this ancient city, but as none of them ever made it out again and the endlessly shifting sands quickly covered any traces they might have left, there was no way of knowing whether this was true, or what underground entrances they might have stumbled upon.

We were now certain that the most important part of the kingdom lay beneath our feet, yet we couldn't find a way in. Frustration blazed in our minds. Finally, by studying each street and building carefully, looking closely from our perch at every single structure, we noticed that one of the stone houses was slightly taller than the ones around it, a fact we could easily have missed because that house too had a layer of sand obscuring its outlines.

That was the only clue we had, so we quickly clambered down and went over to the house. Close up, it appeared to be a temple, also carved of Zaklaman black stone, the entrance made to look like the mouth of some gigantic beast. There was so much sand that Kai and I had to dig a tunnel before we could enter. Everyone put on their gas masks, just in case, and with flares illuminating our path, we slowly made our way inside.

Past the opening, we found ourselves in a vast cavern with eight stone columns to either side. The sand that completely blocked the entrance had also acted as a seal, so the interior was completely clear—not a grain to be seen.

At the farthest end of the hall from us was a single eyeball, this time carved from jade. Unnervingly, the stone was naturally threaded with red, while the pupil was a clear, piercing blue, looking alarmingly realistic.

I couldn't find my tongue. Silently, I crept closer. Although my first thought had been how valuable this artifact might be, as I went up to it and touched it, I thought it was worth this whole cursed trip into the desert just to catch a glimpse of such a sacred object. If I hadn't seen it for myself, I'd never have dared imagine something so precious could exist.

Untroubled by such thoughts, Kai stretched out a hand and made a grab for the jade eye, intending to stuff it into his backpack. He struggled with all his might, but the carving seemed rooted to the floor and didn't shift even an inch.

Afraid Kai would damage the item with his brute force, the professor hastily shoved him aside, and scolded him for even touching it. Meanwhile, Julie noticed an odd-shaped indentation in the statue. "Hang on," she said. "Kai, it looks like your family heirloom medallion might fit in here. Give it a go. Maybe it's some kind of key."

Kai was overjoyed. He pulled the jade piece from his pocket and held it over the aperture. "If this fits, then this eyeball belongs to me," he declared. "If the rest of you want a piece, you'll have to fight me for it. Look at it. All mine. Brother Hu, we've struck it rich this time."

CHAPTER THIRTEEN

APART FROM ME, EVERYONE IN THE ROOM WAS BAFFLED BY KAI'S words. What was wrong with him? you could see them thinking. How could this jade eyeball suddenly belong to him?

I hurried over. "If we let this crowd discover we're actually gold hunters, they might turn against us. Shush!" I whispered in Kai's ear. Then I pretended to smack him on the head. "No need to make jokes like that. Why don't you hurry up and try your medallion? Don't keep us waiting."

Realizing he'd said the wrong thing, Kai obediently shut his mouth. Fortunately, he was still wearing his gas mask, so no one could see his facial expression, which at least made the whole situation a little less awkward.

Professor Chen and his bookworm students seemed

oblivious, so I was mainly worried about Julie realizing what we actually were. Her brain was sharp. The slightest slip and she'd be on to us. Or maybe she'd suspected all along that we were grave robbers. In any case, the moment had passed, and there was no need to stress out over it. I turned my attention to helping Kai fit his jade amulet into the indentation in the eyeball.

The eyeball was swiveled upward, as if staring at the ceiling, and the gap was right on top of it. The jagged outline of the space did look like Kai's jade piece would fit into it, and after a little maneuvering, we finally got it slotted into place with a satisfying click. The giant eye twitched, then ponderously rolled away. The floor where it had stood was perfectly smooth, with no indication of what mechanism had kept it so firmly fixed in place.

Scooping up the artifact, I pressed it into the professor's hands, asking him to examine it closely.

Julie lit another flare to give him some light. Professor Chen got out his magnifying glass and turned the eyeball over and over in his hand, shaking his head the whole time. "I—I have no idea what its function is," he said. "A jade eye the size of a human head. It looks completely natural, with no trace of human handiwork. In fact, I'm pretty certain that two thousand years ago, no technology on earth could have produced an object like this."

The Jingjue civilization really was shrouded in mystery. Even after devoting several decades of his life to deciphering it, Professor Chen was barely scratching the surface. At most, he had a beginner's understanding of their language and history. He'd only just learned that this was a society that worshiped eyes, thanks to the black tower totem. It was impossible to know very much about this jade item we'd just come across.

All we could say for certain was that this great stone hall with its sixteen vast columns must be a temple. And of course, if the Jingjue prized the eye above all things, they'd naturally have placed one at the center of their place of worship.

But why was there an indentation that happened to fit Kai's jade amulet exactly? And what mechanism allowed the eyeball to move only when that space was filled? These were mysteries we still had to solve.

Looking stern, Professor Chen asked Kai if he would be so kind as to explain the origins of his jade piece. The complete truth, he urged, not some incredible exaggeration. Just the facts.

This was astute. Obviously, not a soul had believed his story about acquiring the amulet while hunting bandits with his dad, but because it happened to have a few words of the Guidong language on it, they'd agreed to let him join the team and come with us to Xinjiang.

Now that he was being questioned seriously and the eyes of the entire group were on him, Kai had no choice but to admit he didn't know much about its origins. He would tell us what he could.

It all started when Kai's father was a teenager himself. He was in the army when one of his close friends was deployed as a battalion commander into Xinjiang, to take on the rebels on the southwestern border of the Taklimakan Desert. The friend led his troops to Niya, where they encountered more than a hundred bandits.

The situation in Xinjiang at the time was chaotic, with

marauding gangs of bandits and horse thieves everywhere. It was commonplace for the army to get caught up in local skirmishes, which were always short and intense, ending with most of the rebels either dead or fleeing. At Niya, Kai's father's friend found this jade amulet on the body of a bandit with a mighty black beard. There was no indication of the history or function of the artifact, but as it was an unusual color and there were strange symbols on it, he was captivated and decided to keep it.

Many years later, when he heard that his old comrade in arms had a new baby boy, he thought this jade piece would make a good gift and sent it over.

Kai's father died when Kai was just a little boy, and didn't have much to leave to him, so this jade amulet was one of the few family treasures left. The family friend had passed away too, so it was no good looking there. And that was all he knew about it, Kai said, concluding his account.

Professor Chen sighed. "It's a shame all these people are no longer with us," he said. "After it's passed through so many hands, it's impossible to say where this jade piece first came from." He continued muttering to himself, in real distress at being unable to pinpoint the origin of this mystical artifact.

Julie took the jade eyeball from him and had a close look herself. Noticing how fully it absorbed her attention, I thought back to how she'd barely spoken a word since we'd entered Jingjue City, and wondered if seeing these ruins was making her remember her father, and if she was sad at not having discovered a single trace of him yet. Mr. Yang and his team had disappeared more than a year ago, and we didn't even know if they'd made it as far as we had. Besides, the winds whistling through the mountain pass were so strong that sand was constantly gusting over this city, burying and then uncovering it countless times each year. Anything we found on this trip we would find out of sheer luck. Looking for a small group of people in this vast desert was like trying to find a needle at the bottom of the ocean. Julie must have been clutching on to a whisper of hope that she'd finally discover her father's fate. But the deeper we traveled into the ruins, the fainter the possibilities grew and the more disappointed she must have been.

Julie had saved my life back in the valley, and I was determined to do something for her in return. Seeing how enraptured she was by this artifact, I wished the amulet belonged to me. If it had been mine, I'd have given it to her immediately.

Before Julie had finished studying the eyeball, Kai grew anxious and reached out for it. Julie took a step back. "What's your hurry?" she snapped at him. "I'll return it when I'm done."

"Right," he retorted. "This jade piece is a family heirloom. I think I'd better take it back now." And with that, he reached out to snatch it.

I quickly placed myself between them. "Please, both of you, there's no need to fight. You're making me look bad. As the leader of this expedition, I'll make the decisions here. How about letting Miss Yang have another five minutes with the eyeball?"

My biggest worry was that they would start tussling and end up dropping it. Instead, the opposite happened—seeing me intervene, they both pulled back their hands at the same time. I quickly reached out, but the thing was so smooth and round, I failed to get a grip on it and could only watch as it tumbled heavily to the ground, shattering into eight segments.

"You clumsy fools!" Professor Chen exploded. He wagged a finger at all of us. "What have you done?"

All at once, we were gabbling, gesturing wildly. "I didn't . . . We didn't mean . . . I only wanted to . . . We didn't expect . . . How could this break so easily?" I bent down and picked up the fragments, praying that we'd be able to somehow glue them back together. But it became clear the eyeball was damaged beyond repair.

"Forget it, Tianyi," said Kai. "What's done is done!" He took my arm and pulled me to my feet.

Standing upright so suddenly made me dizzy, and I tumbled backward, landing on my back. As I struggled up, my head tilted and I saw something we'd all missed: on the ceiling of this temple was an eye about the size of a large basin, glistening as it stared down at us.

I quickly pointed my flashlight upward. The ceiling was high here but should still have been within reach of my beam. Yet the darkness seemed to swallow every speck of light, so there was nothing to be seen but that enormous bloodshot eye, floating in a sea of blackness.

Now that their attention was drawn to it, the others turned and ran for the entrance, afraid of what the eye might do now that it had seen us.

In that instant, the giant eye rotated in midair, then swiftly plummeted to the ground. At closer range, it revealed itself to be a translucent, fleshy globe, a milky-white surface filled with a clump of some sort of dark material. No wonder it had looked like an eyeball from a distance.

Seeing this strange object draw closer, Kai panicked and pulled out his rifle. I grabbed his arm. "Careful!" I shouted.

Before I could say any more, the fleshy object burst apart with a ripping sound, revealing hundreds of those strange black snakes, miniature versions of the one we'd seen in the Zaklaman valley, all tangled together, inky scales covering their tiny bodies, tumorlike hoods over their heads.

The snakes lay in little heaps, their writhing bodies still covered in translucent fluid from the egg they'd just hatched from. It was a revolting sight. All our stomachs turned, and we immediately took a few steps back.

I suddenly remembered the half-man, half-snake statue we'd seen. Its head had been covered with a similar black sphere, which the professor had been certain was some sort of eye. No wonder Julie had been able to save my life in the valley by distracting the snake with a beam of light. Even if that fleshy hood wasn't an eye, it was definitely extremely sensitive to light.

There was no time to waste. While the snakes were still tangled up, Kai and I quickly jumped in front of the others and turned our guns on the creatures. Knowing how resilient they were, able to fatally wound a person even if only their heads were left, I shouted to Chu Jian as I fired to fling the solid fuel at them and burn their remains to ashes.

The flames illuminated every corner of the vast stone hall. Hundreds of snakes sizzled before they'd even had a chance to bare their venomous fangs. As they were reduced to nothing, I let out a long breath. Luckily, we'd acted fast. But had the snakes appeared because we smashed the jade eyeball? Or had we unwittingly carried out a holy ritual by inserting the amulet into the eyeball, drawing the snakes here from some other dimension? Whatever the answer, we'd have to be very careful if any more of these eye totems showed up.

I ordered the group to scan every inch of the floor, in case we'd missed any of the tiny snakes. Meanwhile, I studied the ceiling, which had now reverted to regular stone slabs. There was no indication of where the serpent egg might have come from.

Our inspection reassured us that we were safe for now, but it did turn up one other discovery. Each of the sixteen stone columns had six carvings of eyes on it, and each had a hexagonal base, with a small insignia on each side: a hungry ghost, a herd animal, a plainsman, a giant-eyed figure, a guardian beast, and one blank side.

Professor Chen carefully noted down the positions of these symbols, sketching them quickly in his notebook, then instructed us to try rotating the hexagonal base. We put our shoulders into it and realized that sure enough, these were actually rings around the main column, and with enough force, they could be moved.

The professor said this made it clear we were in a temple, and what's more, one with multiple functions—the symbols on the stone pillars could be swiveled, changing the purpose of the room.

The pillars were in clumps of four, and the symbols were set so the guardians were at the fore. Even if the jade eye was a holy object and Kai's amulet had started off some kind of mechanism, it didn't mean other rituals couldn't exist in this space. But as for how the jade eyeball had come to manifest itself, that might be a question we'd never be able to answer.

Maybe previous grave robbers or archaeologists had somehow fumbled it from its hiding place, or maybe the slaves who rebelled against the Jingjue queen two thousand years ago had left it behind in their haste. We would never know.

"Professor, this temple seems to be just as important a site as the palace," Julie said. "What if there's a tunnel leading to the palace itself here? Should we look for one? Little Ye still isn't well. If we find one, we'll be able to get her to the water source quickly."

Professor Chen nodded. "I'd wager that there is a tunnel, yes, but it's surely a well-hidden one. Look how big this place is—how will we ever find it?"

"That's easy," Kai chimed in. "You paid us to clear the way for you, remember? Tianyi and I got hold of all those explosives, so we can blast a new tunnel for you."

"Absolutely not!" exclaimed the professor, frantically waving the suggestion away. "You will do nothing of the sort. These are the last traces of an ancient civilization. It would be barbaric to harm even one brick of this place."

The shattered jade eye still on my mind, I thought this might be my opportunity to redeem myself. I remembered every single thing the manual said about the veins of the land and the paths of feng shui, and I was pretty sure I'd be able to find any secret tunnels that might be around.

"The way I see it, the arrangement of these sixteen pillars exactly matches the positions of the sixteen underground dragons," I said calmly. "This corresponds to the constellation of the Vast Door. Many tombs from the Han dynasty make use of such a device. And earlier, from the top of the black tower, we saw that the layout of this city is in keeping with the highest principles of geomancy, showing that the queen must have been very learned in metaphysics. So why don't I try using the golden acupoints to find any hidden exits? I don't have a lot of experience, but if I don't succeed, we can always think of some other plan."

Everyone agreed that there was no harm in trying, and so the group stood by quietly, waiting to see what I would do. I walked into the middle of the temple and studied the space. With only sixteen columns, there weren't too many possible permutations, and after walking around them several times, I thought I had the measure of the place.

These sixteen dragons were actually snakes. The manual states that the flowing of snakes inevitably leads north to south. Of these sixteen pathways, only one was a true dragon. I've made it sound easy, but in practice it took a lot of calculation before I was able to find my target: a group of four stone slabs at the far end of the hall.

Carefully tapping at them with an archaeologist's chisel, I verified that three of these were the real thing, while the forth one gave out a hollow echo. The slab was about half a foot long, with no sign of any opening mechanism. It would seem this passageway hadn't been used very often, and I didn't see how we would gain access without using explosives. Unless . . . the closest pillar controlled it. But would it still work?

I called Kai over to help turn the hexagonal base. We'd need to be very careful—one false move, and who knew what might be unleashed on us next. Just to be sure, I asked Professor Chen and the others to head back outside. Then, wiping away the sweat on my brow, I told Kai that we should very slowly swivel the blank side to face the slab that I suspected covered the tunnel. Next, we'd have to rotate it five spaces clockwise, back one, then another eleven spaces clockwise, and finally back two. Not one more or less.

"Do you think I can't count?" grumbled Kai. "I've got it. Enough talking—let's get moving!"

In my mind, I silently ran through the secret mantra "Dragons from a thousand miles, all around us, five steps toward yang, one toward yin."

With all our might, the two of us moved the base of the pillar, counting out loud to make sure we got the combination right. As the last side rotated into place, we heard an enormous grinding noise, and the stone slab toppled into nothingness, revealing a tunnel stretching into endless darkness.

CHAPTER FOURTEEN

I LET OUT A SIGH OF RELIEF. WE'D MANAGED TO GET THE TUNNEL open without attracting any more unwelcome company. Shining my flashlight into its depths, I saw a staircase carved out of black stone snaking down. My light wasn't particularly powerful, though, so the illumination didn't reach all the way to the bottom.

Kai waved to summon back the other five, who'd been waiting by the entrance. They hurried over, full of praise for my feng shui skills.

I humbly thanked them, then said we should get moving. It was already past noon. I told them we should drink some water and have a quick meal to fortify ourselves, then leave behind as much of our equipment as possible. There was no knowing how deep this tunnel was, so we might as well prepare for a long journey.

As we were chewing on our rations, Sa Dipeng asked me how on earth I'd managed to locate the one stone slab that concealed our path.

"It was obvious from the positioning of these sixteen columns," I told him. "This is all according to the Vast Door constellation—you know where the name comes from? It's because this configuration is often used to hide entrances. It's based on a Luo mathematical formula, derived in turn from the map of the stars. But there are deeper mysteries at work here, and I'm afraid if I say too much it'll only confuse you."

After a quick rest, the group was ready for me to lead them beneath the temple. Just under the opening, we found a lever that opened the stone slab from the inside. It was an ingenious mechanism, and it worked perfectly well even after two thousand years. Although it was designed on the basis of complex mathematical calculations, the actual structure was simple enough to have remained functional all this time. If this was the doing of the Jingjue queen, then she must have been a supernaturally talented woman.

We were worried about the possibility of hidden traps, so we proceeded with great caution, spacing ourselves out and taking slow steps. Finally, we got to the bottom of the stairs, and before our eyes was a passage about fifteen feet wide and nine feet high.

The walls here were no longer black stone, but were built from typical Western Region bricks, made from a mixture of sand, soil, and cow dung. The tunnel rose to an arch above our heads, and on the walls were brightly colored paintings, a series of bizarre images.

Since the Jingjue people treated eyes as a totem, a great number appeared in this passage from the temple: large and small, open and shut, sometimes as stark eyeballs, other times complete with lids and lashes. I imagined only priests and the queen herself would have had the privilege to enter here.

The professor and his students couldn't take their eyes off those walls. They were gaping with wonder.

Professor Chen told us that the ruins discovered by foreign archaeologists in the early nineteenth century also contained giant wall murals, mostly of religious subjects, but unfortunately, the government of the time didn't do enough to protect them. They all ended up getting stolen and shipped overseas. Yet here was a perfectly preserved specimen, one from the most ancient, most mysterious of the Western Regions' thirty-six kingdoms. This discovery would surely send shock waves around the world.

Hearing the professor talk, I remembered the legend about the queen being a demon. This city was so spooky that I was starting to wonder if there was any truth to that, and I wanted to be as well prepared as possible. Pulling out my flashlight, I studied the pictures more closely.

The strange thing was, despite the number of paintings along this underground passage, not one depicted the queen. Many of them showed the same sequence of events: a jade eyeball emanating light, a black hole appearing in the air above it, and an egg shaped like a giant eye dropping out of that void. Some also showed countless monstrous black snakes climbing from their egg, sinking their fangs into slaves whose hands and feet were bound.

There were also landscapes of the black mountains, with more of those snakes slithering down the slopes, and herds of wild animals on bended knee, bowing in worship to those strange creatures.

We'd just experienced some of those scenes ourselves. Seeing them all laid out like this, we thought Professor Chen must be right, and those bizarre black snakes must have been treated as guardian beasts by the inhabitants of Jingjue. The people knew how to summon and control these creatures, and even offered them human beings as living sacrifices. Who would have thought that a thousand years after the Jingjue Kingdom was buried beneath the shifting sands, these snakes would still be in existence?

We'd been walking along as we examined the pictures, but our footsteps halted at the final image: an enormous hole in the ground, with a narrow staircase winding down its sides.

Julie turned to the professor. "Do you think this could have anything to do with the origins of the Guidong tribe?" she asked him. "After all, *guidong* means 'ghost-hole.'"

"It's possible," he replied. "Look how narrow those steps are. They're out of proportion with the hole. And something so big, tunneling straight down into the earth, couldn't have been created by humankind. Could this be the ghost-hole?"

I remembered hearing the legend that the Guidong tribe had appeared from underground, but at the time I'd thought it must just be the ancient people talking nonsense. Looking at these pictures now, I wondered if I'd been wrong. The murals weren't just scenes made up to scare people; we'd witnessed some of them come true with our own eyes. For all we knew, deep within this city, we really would find a gigantic hole like this.

Kai laughed. "There couldn't be a hole as big as this anywhere in the world," he said. "Unless you think it reaches all the way across the globe?"

Julie ignored him and kept questioning the professor. "Those statues with giant eyes—could it be that this is what the Guidong tribe originally looked like? And if they used to live in the darkness of underground, no wonder they found eyes so important."

"That's one theory," acknowledged the professor, "but there are other possibilities. This giant hole is something that appears again and again in the Guidong civilization. It's the unreal space you talked about, but in physical form. In ancient times, when the Guidong people found this, they'd have been unable to understand why such an enormous hole would exist in the world. They worshiped the power of the natural world, and might have taken this as evidence of the divine at work. They longed for their eyes to become more powerful so they could see to the bottom of the hole. Then some people probably claimed they could see the world that lay at the bottom, and they were elevated by society, eventually becoming rulers or priests. Their eyes were the source of their power, so vision became a form of strength."

Kai stood openmouthed as he listened to the professor speak. "Nice one, old man," he said, giving Professor Chen a big thumbs-up. "You make it sound like all this actually happened. You should have a market stall. With a tongue like yours, you'd be able to sell ice to Eskimos."

Professor Chen was clearly in no mood to joke with him, and answered tartly, "It's just a hypothesis. I can't say for certain. Why don't we get out of this tunnel and see if we can find a giant hole? Nothing like the evidence of our own senses."

For some reason, hearing them talk about the giant hole made me remember a story I'd heard from my grandfather about a nine-story underground demon pagoda he'd found in the Kunlun Mountains. Quite a few of his comrades had died during that adventure. Thinking of that tale, I worried what would happen if there were some accident now. If we hadn't needed to go into the palace to find a source of water, I'd have been tempted to drag them all back. After all, we'd already made one important discovery on this expedition. There was no need to go any farther.

I turned to the professor. "Let's not take too many risks," I said. "All of you have important positions in society. There's no need to put yourselves in danger. After we refill our water containers in the palace, we should go back. We've found the Jingjue Kingdom. Our task is done. Why not just put all this in a report to the authorities and let the government deal with whatever comes next?"

Professor Chen shook his head but said nothing. His whole life, he'd wanted to plunge into the mysteries of the Guidong civilization, and now he was finally here. Of course it must have been scratching at his heart to find the answers. Besides, Julie was convinced that her father and his team had been to Jingjue, and she was determined to search every corner of this place for traces of them. I didn't think I'd be able to convince her to turn back either.

So I had no choice but to forge ahead with them.

The tunnel wasn't particularly long. At the other end, we found not a staircase, as I'd expected, but a stone pillar, with no sign of a door.

Kai studied the wall blocking our path, then turned to me. "Tianyi," he whispered, "do you have any tricks up your sleeve? If not, we'll have to bust out the dynamite."

"Do you have to blow up everything in your way?" I snapped. "Use your brain. Let's have a closer look. I bet there's a secret mechanism in this pillar."

This pillar was many times smaller than the sixteen giant columns in the temple, but it was proportioned exactly the same, down to the carved hexagon at its base. The empty side faced the dead-end wall.

This had to be the tail of the sixteen dragons above. Getting Kai to help me, I turned the base according to the manual, reversing the "dragon summoning" ritual to get the "dragon shaking" charm.

As we turned the final panel into place, the mud-brick wall in front of us obligingly split open. Kai went first, rifle at the ready, and the rest of us followed single file.

Once we were all safely out of the passage, we got out our flashlights and studied our surroundings. Even though we were still beneath the surface, this was an imposing hall. The paint and decorative carvings had long since eroded away, but we could still tell how magnificent it must once have been. We were surely in the underground palace.

This seemed to be the main reception room. The tunnel let us out behind a throne carved from jade, and as the door swung shut behind us, we appreciated how well it was constructed; once it closed, it was impossible to tell there was any kind of secret entrance there.

And so we'd finally arrived at the Jingjue Imperial Palace, which up to that moment had seemed to exist only in legends. To see as clearly as possible, we made use of every form of illumination we were carrying, throwing light in all directions. We were in a vast chamber, with both the floor and that enormous throne made entirely of jade. Several of the chains holding up the ceiling lamps had snapped, and these now lay sprawled and broken on the ground. Sand mice skittered about in the corners, suggesting that the air here was breathable. Although the jade had survived intact, the other artifacts—ceramics, wood, iron, bronze, and silk—had not weathered as well, and were in a state of advanced deterioration.

The best-preserved object was the throne, which had an eyeball made of red jade set into its back. Inlaid gold and silver filigree covered the rest of the throne's surface, with misty mountains and all kinds of animals intricately carved into it. The seat was the hue of sheep's milk, eye-catching in this giant, mostly dark-colored chamber.

Kai looked disappointed. He slumped onto the throne and thumped his hand on the armrest. "This is the only thing here worth a cent," he said glumly. "As for the rest of this stuff, we might as well call the recycling center to come pick it up."

That was Kai all over: absolutely no sense of how to behave. No discipline. Trying to lighten the mood, I said, "But, Kai, don't forget that you're one of the common people. Don't start getting all high and mighty sitting up there."

"Ha!" Kai chuckled. "I'm just getting a feel for this throne.

It might be worth a million dollars. Shame the top bit is so big; we'll probably have to break it apart to transport it."

"Let's not worry about moving it," I hastily broke in. "You won't believe me, but I'm telling you, this jade throne is where the Jingjue queen once sat, and for all we know, her spirit may still be roaming around this palace, all lonely after thousands of years on her own. She might even catch a sight of you and think, 'Mmm, what a nice companion that chubby boy would make.' Before you know it, you'll be going steady with an undead queen. She always gets her way, you know."

This little speech was enough to give Kai a fright. Unfortunately, the others heard it too. Little Ye had recovered enough to take small steps, but hearing that the dead queen's vengeful spirit might still be on the premises, her eyeballs rolled back and she fainted dead away again.

Julie flew into a spitting rage. "Could the two of you stop talking nonsense? It's hardly the time. Now look what you've done—aren't you going to come help?"

Seeing that we'd blundered again, Kai and I didn't dare argue but hurried over to lift Little Ye off the floor and onto Kai's back. It would have been great if he'd kept quiet at this point, but of course he had to have the last word. "Going steady with the undead queen, huh? I've never met anyone as uncultured as you. Queens don't go steady. They have—what do you call them?—imperial consorts."

"I think you mean eunuchs," Julie said acidly.

I stifled a laugh. The mood was still somber after Hao Aiguo's death, and it really wouldn't have been appropriate— though who knew Julie Yang had a sense of humor too? I split the group up into teams of two, and we walked through the large hall, searching for any signs that might point us toward a water source.

The Jingjue Kingdom's underground palace wasn't as large as I'd imagined. The throne room was certainly impressive, but the antechambers on either side were cramped. The main entrance and stairs were completely buried under sand, but an area of the black stone roof near the door had been blown up, indicating that at least one set of explorers had already made their way in here. Probably several decades ago. Maybe the man in the black-and-white photograph? In any case, the gap had long since been filled by the desert.

Examining the two side rooms and finding nothing, I turned to the rear quarters. This was where the royal family would have lived, and scattered around the space were a number of fountains surrounded by jade railings. Unfortunately, the fountains had all dried out a long time ago. We walked along single file, keeping a sharp eye out, until Julie suddenly called, "Listen, do you hear running water?"

I pricked up my ears, and sure enough, there was a liquid burbling not too far away. It was coming from the direction of the bedchambers. We started walking faster, following the sound, and ended up in a cave that opened out behind the palace.

The ground began sloping downward here, leading us farther underground. We finally found ourselves in a natural cavern about the size of a soccer field. It might not have been man-made, but man had definitely altered it—all the surfaces were smooth, and there was an artificial lake in its center, not too large, with a little bump of land in the middle, an island no more than thirty-five feet square. The water was so calm it could have been a mirror, and a path ran all around it.

For more than a week, we'd had nothing to drink but our foul-tasting water. The small ration would have left us thirsty in our regular lives, let alone in the middle of the desert. Seeing this crystalline lake, it was all we could do not to run over and plunge our heads right into it, but Julie stopped us.

"The water source might have gotten cut off," she explained, "and stagnant water becomes poisonous. Underground rivers change their course all the time, and the water here might be different from two thousand years ago. The soil in the Western Regions contains lots of chemicals, like nitrites and sulfates. For all we know, there might be all kinds of dissolved toxins here. Let's be careful."

Drawing closer, I saw some movement. It was hundreds of tiny fish, their tails glittering as they moved. I smiled. "No need to worry," I said. "The water must be fine—otherwise these little guys would be floating belly up."

As soon as the words were out, the rest of the group charged forward and began taking huge swigs of water, not stopping until their stomachs were bulging out. Even then, they still felt they hadn't drunk enough, and some didn't stop till they were literally dribbling from the mouth.

Little Ye had to go easy, so Julie salted some water in a bottle and fed it to her drop by drop. The rest of us slumped by the lakeside, too full to even think about moving.

I'd never imagined water could taste so delicious. Now I sprawled on the ground, my limbs outstretched, my eyes shut. In the underground silence, I thought I heard water flowing

148

somewhere. But that made sense: this placid lake couldn't have produced the burbling sound we'd heard earlier. It was coming from farther off, from a much larger body of water, maybe the hidden Zidu River, which was said to wind around the Zaklaman Mountains.

Just as my thoughts were wandering even further, Julie nudged my shoulder and pointed at the outcropping in the center of the lake. I turned to look. The others had been roused too, and we gaped together at an unimaginable sight.

Without us noticing, tiny insects had swarmed onto the island, covering it in a bright green carpet. There must have been more than ten thousand of the critters. As we watched, their bodies faded to ashy gray, and one by one they wriggled from their outer shells. Their new bodies glimmered with luminescence, like stars gathered from the night sky. Soon they would be strong enough to spread their folded wings and soar skyward.

At that moment, large mice scurried from all corners of the cavern. They ignored us as they ran right past, plunging without hesitation into the water, paddling their way across, scrabbling onto the island, and greedily shoveling the newly hatched creatures into their mouths. It was a scene of carnage. In just a few seconds, they'd gobbled up every one of those exquisite insects.

The notion that they must do this all the time turned my stomach, and I was violently sick. Fortunately, there was nothing in my belly but lake water, and it all gushed out.

Satiated, the mice made their way back to shore and dispersed once again into the darkness.

Chu Jian picked up a stone and was about to fling it at

one of the stragglers, but I caught his arm. In gratitude to my grandfather's benefactor, my family had a rule that no Hu would ever allow a mouse to be harmed. These creatures had no quarrel with us; we might as well let them be.

"Disgusting," spat Kai. "This lake is full of mice. Who knows how much mouse fur we drank with our water. I bet they pee in it too."

"Stop talking about it," I said, "or I might vomit again. Anyway, there's no point staying here. Let's move on."

Indeed, no one in the group wanted to touch a drop more of this water, so we continued deeper into the cave. There were no other paths, just a single passageway with the sound of a flowing river coming from its other end.

As we drew closer, the air became ever more full of moisture, and the walls grew damp. Along this stretch, man-made rooms began appearing to either side, all fitted with metal bars locked up tight. In each of these cells was a selection of torture instruments—it would seem this was where prisoners had once been punished. Now they'd turned into mouse nests, and black mouse poop was everywhere on the floor.

A few hundred yards on, we finally arrived at the end of the path, where a river rushed past, as it no doubt had for thousands of years. This was the Zidu River, which had never run dry in all its existence. Not only was it wide, it also ran deep. At its end, it would meet and combine with the Tarim.

All the rivers of the Xinjiang Desert had one thing in common: no matter how large the volume of water, they were never able to burst from the confines of the desert and reach the ocean. Instead, both the interior surface rivers and the subterranean ones gradually petered out, swallowed by the desert.

An even larger cave stood on the opposite shore, connected to us by a bridge—again, carved out of black stone from the Zaklaman Mountains. Reaching out gracefully, the dark arc curved over the rushing waters of the Zidu River.

In front of the cave was an enormous metal gate, which was raised and lowered by chains the thickness of a human arm. It was half closed, propped open at the bottom by an enormous boulder. We tried to see past into the path ahead, but it remained stubbornly dark and unfathomable. Impossible to say what lay in wait for us.

"My word," said Professor Chen. "When we saw that someone had blasted a hole in the underground palace, I thought surely someone had been here before us. And see how thick this gate is? It's in the deepest reaches of the third story belowground, which surely means the Jingjue queen's final resting place is at the end of this path."

What Professor Chen said made perfect sense. The only thing was, we all suspected that this was too easy. Other archaeologists had made their way into this palace, and the cave was hardly concealed, so surely we weren't the first ones here. Could it be that all our predecessors had made their way into the burial site, only to die there?

I asked the professor what he thought—was it worth taking the risk and going in? "Yes!" he answered without hesitation. "We have to at least take a look, to make sure the Jingjue queen's tomb hasn't been robbed or damaged. If I could just see it once, I'd die happy. And if my old bones end up buried here, well, that's fair enough. By the time you get to my age, you really don't care much about anything. But you kids are still young, so I'll understand if you'd rather hang back. I can go on alone."

Julie was fiddling with the settings on her camera. "Of course I'm going in," she said, not even looking up. Her voice was deadpan, as if she'd never considered the possibility of doing anything else and the only question in her mind was whether to be the first or second person to enter.

Seeing how stubborn they looked, I knew I'd have to follow them. I'd never be able to forgive myself if anything happened to either of them.

I told Kai to stay behind and take care of the three students, but he shook his head. "So I get to be the babysitter? No thank you. I'm just going to spend all my time worrying about the three of you. If anyone's going in, then we should all stick together. Otherwise, let's turn back now." He leaned into my ear and whispered. "You can relax. I promise not to steal any gold or jewels, no matter how much tempting treasure we might see in there."

The students agreed with Kai. They weren't about to miss out on such an amazing opportunity—not after trekking hundreds of miles across the blazing desert and suffering all kinds of hardships to reach this place. If anything were to go wrong, surely it would be better to have the entire gang there to help.

If no one wanted to stay behind, then what were we going to do with Little Ye, who hadn't fully recovered? But she took a swig of cold salt water and seemed to get a momentary burst of energy, proclaiming, "I'm not going to be left behind either. I'm coming in with you."

We were in trouble now. Kai and I were more than capable, but we couldn't take care of five helpless bookworms between us if something disastrous really happened. Only Chu Jian, who was pretty brawny, might be able to lend a hand. But otherwise—

"How about this?" I told the group. "I'll go in first and have a look. If I don't come back after a few hours, then you should definitely not come after me."

"No way!" yelped Kai. "If you're going in, then so am I. It's safer that way."

I patted him on the shoulder. "I'll be fine on my own. Don't worry about me. But if something does go wrong, I'll need you here to get the others safely back home."

Julie rolled her eyes. "Done being heroes, you two? I'm coming in now."

I couldn't believe my ears. "Fine," I said. "But if this is some kind of trap, I might not be able to save myself. Don't expect me to take care of you too."

"Who knows which of us will end up taking care of the other?" she retorted. "Anyway, I can't let you go in there alone. If there's danger, we'll face it together." With that, she grabbed the rifle out of Kai's hands and quickly pulled open the chamber to check that it was loaded, then cocked it at the ready. I was left gaping at her. She handled her weapon like an expert. I'd never have pegged our Miss Yang as a sharpshooter.

As we were quickly repacking our gear, Kai whispered to me, "Hey, Tianyi, I've noticed there's something strange about the way Julie looks at you. Do you think she likes you?"

I smacked him on the head. "There must be something wrong with your eyes. I haven't seen anything like that, and I think I'd have noticed. She's not my type, anyway. Besides, if I wound up dating a foreigner, my dad would probably break my legs."

"All right, then," said Kai. "I was worried you were falling for her. I can't stand people with money. It doesn't make her the boss of us. Just make sure you don't get taken in by her."

I strapped on all the guns and explosives we'd scavenged from the bandits in the valley and made sure I had all my spare ammo and tools, new batteries in the flashlight, and a charm to ward off evil in my hand. "May the powers that be protect us," I murmured.

Julie was ready too. She asked if I had any idea what the layout of the tomb might be. "Impossible to tell from the outside," I told her. "I'd need to look at the contours of the land, the positions of the stars, the acupoints and ley lines. All those feng shui details might indicate when this was built and what structure was used. If only we weren't underground. Nothing I've studied has prepared me for this. A bridge over water that leads to a tomb goes against every principle of feng shui. As for what's on the other side, it's anyone's guess. We'll just have to be careful and definitely not touch anything that looks like it might trigger some mechanism. They've probably booby-trapped the place. Keep an eye out for those weird black snakes too. You know how fast they move. If they get too close, we're done for."

Julie nodded and positioned herself to be the first over the black stone bridge. I followed closely behind her, and as the other five watched, the two of us reached the other side of the water and squeezed through the gap beneath that ominous gate.

CHAPTER FIFTEEN

ON THE OTHER SIDE OF THE PORTAL, A LONG, NARROW PATH SNAKED its way downward. When Julie flung a flare ahead of us, it rolled down the steep slope for quite some time before stopping. Its glow was a speck in the distance, barely detectable.

I drew in a sharp breath. If this really was the way to the tomb, it was much longer than I'd expected. At least there weren't any corpses along the way, as far as I could tell. If this passageway was a trap, those who'd gone before us would surely have left some mark.

Even so, we couldn't afford to be careless. I studied our surroundings carefully with every step. Something definitely seemed off, but I couldn't put my finger on what exactly was wrong.

It was Julie who worked it out. "Have you noticed," she said, "ever since we came in here, there hasn't been a single sign of any mice?"

I nodded. "You're right. And that's odd. The gate is half open and the stone bridge connects this place to the other side—so where are they? The palace was full of them. There's not a scrap of fur to be seen, and I don't smell any mouse pee. I bet their animal instincts warn them to stay away."

Julie didn't respond for a while, just kept walking. Then, out of nowhere, she turned around and faced me. "Tell me the truth, will you? I need to know if you've ever been a grave robber."

Her question caught me off guard, and I couldn't find any words to respond. Even though we were here as part of an archaeological expedition, and even though I saw little difference between archaeologists and tomb robbers, the two groups were like oil and water, insisting on sticking to their own sides and refusing to acknowledge what they had in common. I thought I'd kept a lid on my real profession. How had she seen through me?

Watching me hesitate, Julie nodded. "I was just guessing, actually. You're so familiar with all that old-school feng shui stuff that no one knows about anymore, and you're certainly no stranger to ancient tombs. Look at you. You fit in so well here you could be in your own backyard. That seemed to me like someone with a history of being a robber."

So she didn't know for sure! I cursed her inwardly. All this time I'd been worried about the path being trapped when I should have been on the defense against my travel companion instead.

"My grandfather handed down family secrets to me," I said. "He was the feng shui master at Shiliba Village, helping folk with their supernatural problems. My dad's been a policeman all his life and never learned any of this. It was just a hobby to me, till now. I'm a nerd, really. I get obsessed with things, and I study them as much as possible, tracing everything back to their roots." Chattering on, I managed to change the subject, drawing her attention away from the risky subject of grave robbing. Hopefully, she'd forget it had ever come up.

We walked a long time before finally reaching the bottom of the slope. It ended suddenly in a steep drop, plummeting down to a platform, every inch of which was covered with hundreds of statues, all depicting the same humanoid figures with massive eyes. To the sides, the walls rose into steep cliffs, and looking overhead, we couldn't make out the ceiling, only pitch darkness.

The cavern we were now in was huge—impossible to tell how big exactly, but certainly beyond the range of our flashlights. Was this the end of the road? Yet no matter how carefully we looked, it didn't look anything like the underground tomb depicted in the murals.

"Maybe the queen's coffin is even farther down," Julie said. "The Jingjue people might have destroyed the passage to the tomb, making sure that her rest would never be disturbed."

That seemed plausible. "Just as well," I said, smiling. "So let's head back to—" Before I could finish, Julie had activated three flares and in quick succession flung them far into the space before us, trying to see how deep it was.

We watched the trails of light arc up over the platform,

abruptly hit an obstacle, and drop back to the ground. So the far wall wasn't as distant as I'd thought.

In the remaining light of the flares, we saw that the other end of this chamber held little mounds of what appeared to be gold and silver vessels, pearls and precious stones, and carved jade objects. "Wow!" I exclaimed. "So that's where all the good stuff is. I guess the queen's body must be there too. But how do we get over there?"

Julie had been groping around the edges of the cliff, and now she shook something at me in response. She'd found the edge of a rope ladder, which, when we pulled it, turned out to be suspended from an outcrop of rock, dangling down to the platform below. I tugged at it; it seemed secure enough.

"This might have been left by previous archaeologists," said Julie. "It looks sturdy, but it could be decades old. Probably better to go back and get our own rope ladder."

"That's easily done," I said. "But below us are all kinds of precious objects, jade and jewels and whatnot, so why didn't previous explorers take them away? Lots of foreigners called themselves archaeologists, but you know very well they all came to China as thieves. What kind of thief leaves empty-handed?"

"I get your meaning," Julie replied thoughtfully. "The only way those mounds of treasure could still be untouched is if they were protected by something."

"Exactly. No such thing as a free lunch. The simplest thing always turns out to be the most complicated. Don't you remember Asat Amat talking about the ancient curse on the Black Desert? Anyone taking precious items from this place will end up trapped here forever, buried alive with whatever they coveted."

"Yes." Julie nodded. "That belief is recorded in the *Great Tang Records of the Western Regions* too. The city was called Shalorjara, buried beneath the sands of the Black Desert. But we should be safe from the curse. Professor Chen and the others are respectable scholars; they're not going to start manhandling the artifacts. I'm only worried about your plump friend—maybe you should keep an eye on him."

"What do you mean by that?" I said, getting worked up. "Are you saying Kai and I look like thieves? Just because we're poor doesn't mean we're dishonest. I've given you my word of honor. If I say we won't touch a single item here, then neither of us will so much as lay a finger on anything we see. Maybe you should worry about yourself instead."

Julie's face was white with anger. "Now it sounds like *you're* calling *me* a thief."

Remembering that she'd saved my life, I bit back my furious reply. To be honest, I knew I'd gone too far. I stammered out a grudging apology, and we turned back to join the others. All the way up that steep slope, neither of us said a word, the tension between us thick and ugly.

Professor Chen and the group had been waiting impatiently, and seeing us reappear now, they clamored for details. I filled a water bottle from the river and gulped some down while describing what we'd seen. Julie filled in some of the gaps.

Everyone was thrilled—the scholars at the news of this historical discovery, Kai on hearing about the heaps of gold and silver. Now that we had gotten them excited, no one was willing to stay behind, so the entire expedition came back with us.

I went last, and the second I got past the gate, I must have brushed against it, because the boulder rolled aside and the whole thing came crashing down, sealing us in. After a moment of panic, I remembered we had plenty of explosives with us, so we could probably blast our way out. Luckily, I'd made it all the way in—that thing looked like it weighed a ton! Nothing to be done now, anyway, except to follow the others down the slope, back to the cliff edge.

We quickly got out our rope ladder, fastening it to the same outcrop. I figured no one was going to listen to my warnings at this stage, so I just whispered to Kai that he'd better keep his hands to himself and not pick up so much as the smallest pearl from the treasure heap. I didn't believe in any ancient curse, but I wasn't going to give Julie anything she could use against me. Besides, this was a matter of national pride. She was certainly not going to accuse us Chinese of being thieves again.

"Relax," scoffed Kai. "You can count on me—I won't let you down. I promise not to touch even a mouse dropping." As he turned away, I heard him mutter under his breath, "I'll just come back alone and help myself later."

When the rope ladder was secured, I volunteered to go down first. There were still no mice anywhere about, which at first made me fearful those black snakes might be lurking below. At the bottom, though, all was still and silent. Never mind snakes and mice, there weren't even any insects. Not the tiniest bug anywhere. Along the stone walls were several bronze lanterns, carved to resemble kneeling slaves, their arms outstretched in supplication, holding flames in their hands—except the oil had run out long ago. Looking at this row of exquisitely carved objects, I thought wistfully how any one of them could have sold for a fortune in the marketplace, especially given how ancient they were, and the fame of the city they'd come from.

Standing among these vast heaps of precious stones, I felt my insides churning. I had to fight every last instinct not to shovel all the valuables into my pockets. The only thing I could do was turn my eyes away. Looking up, I whistled to signal that the others should come down too.

As each person descended the rope ladder and turned to face the room, they were stunned into silence by the sight of the riches—so many rare gems and precious metals in all kinds of different styles, making it clear that these had been plundered by the Jingjue from the other kingdoms of the Western Regions. Even Professor Chen couldn't tell us where they all came from. One thing was certain, though: every one was worth more than we'd earn in our entire lifetimes.

Kai's eyes glowed, and I could tell he'd already forgotten the promise he'd made just minutes ago. He reached for the nearest object, a wine jug made from luminescent jade.

I hastily snatched his arm back and muttered in his ear, "Did you think I was joking? You said you'd behave."

He froze. "That was strange! My arm suddenly got a life of its own. It shot out all by itself. I couldn't control it!"

"No excuses," I snapped. "And don't get any ideas." As I spoke, I turned to see if Julie Yang had noticed. Fortunately, she and Chu Jian were busy helping the old professor down the ladder, and she hadn't seen a thing.

"Why are you down here?" I asked Chu Jian. "Didn't we say you'd stay up top to take care of Little Ye?"

"I just wanted to take a look," he replied. "I'll go up again in a sec."

It wasn't just him. Every single one of the group were bug-eyed, looking all around for any sign of the tomb. Despite all the legends about the many dangers that lay in wait for explorers, there was something compelling about this place— something that made it irresistible.

"Let Jian explore a little," Professor Chen said, still panting from the exertion of his climb. "This is a rare educational opportunity. After all their studying, it's good to have my students get some practical experience. No matter how powerful the queen must have been, she's been dead more than two thousand years, and as soon as she was gone, the slaves revolted and brought down her kingdom. We're probably safe. We should be fine as long as everyone remembers their archaeological principles: damage nothing, take nothing."

I thought about it. He had a point—the queen's demonic powers, even if they existed, would surely have died along with her. As for the earlier explorers, maybe they were so dazzled by the treasure that they weighed themselves down and couldn't get out, or became confused and couldn't find the exit. The biggest trap of all was surely these grave goods. But if we kept our heads and didn't pay too much attention to them, we should be all right.

For all the myths that had arisen around the Jingjue queen's life, and despite her mighty kingdom, which was once the terror of the Western Regions, she still passed away in the end. Just like a chessboard, the world is constantly reset for new games, and no matter how much you accomplish and how powerful you are, you can't escape from this law of nature: the board must be cleared, and a new round started.

Now even Little Ye got in on the act, carefully sliding down the ladder with Sa Dipeng's help. We groped our way forward. All around us were dark stone walls. Could we be directly beneath the Zaklaman Mountains?

In such a large space, it was impossible to make out the contours of the surrounding land. We'd so far resisted using our most powerful source of light, in order to conserve its battery, but now seemed like the perfect time to bring it out.

It was a heavy hand-held floodlight, a xenon high-pressure bulb with nickel and platinum as reflectors. When unobstructed, its beams could travel up to a mile and a half. The only thing was, it ran through power like nobody's business, so we'd only be able to use it for a very short time.

While I quickly assembled the apparatus, Kai emptied the batteries out of his waist pouch and loaded them in. Sa Dipeng leaned over to peer shortsightedly at the lens, and Julie quickly pulled him away. "Be careful! This is a very powerful light source. It can blind you from a hundred yards away if you look directly at it."

"Yeah," Kai chimed in, "your eyes would probably explode."

The floodlight only took a few minutes to put together. Telling everyone to stand well behind the light, I flicked the switch and watched as pure radiance shot from it, so strong it might as well have been solid. Sweeping it back and forth, I could finally see what lay all around us.

My first guess had been right—we were definitely beneath the Zaklaman Mountains. Above us and to all sides were great slabs of black stone. Beyond the piles of treasure were countless huge-eyed statues. The floor dropped away beneath them into a precipice. Inching cautiously to the edge and looking down, we saw what lay beneath: an enormous, perfectly circular hole.

It was exactly as depicted in the temple passageway murals. A path wound its way around this unfathomably deep opening. The only human-made modification was a spiral of steps around the perimeter of the hole, leading down into the darkness.

When we pointed the floodlight into the pit, we saw the staircase turn a few rounds and then stop. It would seem there was only so much human technology had been able to do, and the deepest reaches were still unplumbed. Even our powerful light couldn't reach the bottom. I had to pull us back from the edge. I feared that staring down into the murky unknown was liable to leave us so disoriented that we'd find ourselves suddenly taking a step forward, plummeting helplessly into the void.

"This must be the holy ground of the Jingjue," said Julie. "The ghost-hole, *guidong*. But where could it lead?"

I'd been feeling chills through my heart ever since I set eyes on this chasm. "Isn't the legend that it's a portal directly to hell?" I said. "I can't look at it anymore. It's making me dizzy."

"Surely you don't believe in those tales?" Professor Chen said, chuckling. "This is nothing more than an unusually large natural formation. Of course, to the ancients, it must have seemed like the handiwork of the gods, but we ought to be beyond such primitive superstitions."

Kai had been shining the light around the rim, and now

he started yelping for us to come see. He'd found a thin stone column, extending from the cliff face into midair, suspended directly over the giant hole.

Our focus, though, was on where the column ended: a large wooden beam, more than six feet long, that on closer inspection was clearly just an entire tree. Not much had been done to it—several branches stretched from it, some with leaves still clinging to them.

A dozen or so thick chains were shackled around the trunk, fixing it firmly in place. Even more peculiar, some sort of shrub was growing out of the wood, each of its flowers about the size of a bucket, bulbous petals bulging out, then pursing into little mouths. These pouchlike blossoms were jade-green, surrounded by blood-red leaves. This bizarre plant seemed to sprout directly from the tree, its vines winding around the trunk just as the chains did.

I gaped. "This—this is the god-tree of the Kunlun!" I shouted. "My grandfather always told me the wood from a tree's very center was the best thing to make coffins out of. The very finest variety of wood would be from a tree hardly anyone has ever set eyes on, the Kunlun god-tree as described in the ancient books. They say that even removed from soil, water, and sunlight, this tree might stop growing, but will never wither or change its appearance. A corpse in a Kunlun wood coffin won't decay, not even after ten thousand years." I paused and swallowed hard. "Could the Jingjue queen's body be in there?"

"You're right. This must be her tomb," Julie said, her voice trembling. "The legends say this tree is as ancient as the Kunlun hills themselves. They say the first emperor, Qin Shihuang, desired to find it and make his grave from it. Yet it was the Jingjue queen who finally succeeded. This is the best burial place any human being will ever have."

The excitement buzzing among us was palpable. The entire group was about to rush over for a closer look, but the professor hurried to block their way. He looked like he had something urgent to say, but in his agitation he stumbled over a pebble and twisted his ankle.

We helped him up quickly, but he was clearly in pain and couldn't take another step. Finally, we had to sit him back on the ground. "Whatever you do, don't touch anything," he said, grimacing. "Didn't you see the flowers growing out of the coffin?"

"Do you mean those green things?" asked Kai. "What weird plant is that? Those flowers look like giant yams. And whoever heard of a plant growing out of a coffin? Do you think the queen was really a giant seed, and now that they've buried her, she's sprouted?"

The professor kneaded his injured foot. "It's called a corpse bloom, the most precious plant in the world. For all we know, this might be the last specimen left—and it's the most dangerous one as well."

Corpse bloom? The name was enough to send a jolt through us, even though not a single member of the group, Julie included, had heard of such a thing. Desperate to know more, we urged Professor Chen to explain.

"Back in the day, when I was researching the ancient Western Regions civilizations, I saw this flower crop up in the few murals and texts from that period. The corpse bloom seems to have originated during the later Yue era, then sprouted up all along the Silk Road, only to go extinct from the region because it couldn't adapt to the environment. It's said that planting these flowers in a tomb can preserve a corpse forever—and even lend it a special fragrance. This is a treasure. The civilizations of the Western Regions had all kinds of mystical beliefs and religions. Myth and historical reality was so closely intermingled that it's difficult to tell them apart. I hadn't believed this myself, thinking it must be just another story, yet here it is."

Gazing at the distant flowers, Julie asked, "If this plant is as good as all that, why did you say it was the most dangerous thing?"

"Well, the other part of the legend is that the corpse bloom contains an evil spirit," the professor replied. "As soon as it reaches maturity, no living human can come anywhere near it. Rare to find a coffin of Kunlun wood—but that's the only reason we see a corpse bloom thriving in a place like this."

I'd heard many strange stories in my life, but the idea of a symbiotic evil flower-and-coffin was a new one to me. "This is truly strange," I said. "We're deep beneath the Zaklaman Mountains, with no light at all, and yet we find a plant growing. I guess that's exactly what we should expect from the Jingjue queen. We can safely say that we've left the laws of the natural world behind."

CHAPTER SIXTEEN

EVEN AT A DISTANCE, WE COULD CLEARLY DETECT A PUNGENT SCENT. Could the corpse bloom be toxic? Most poisonous plants and animals tend to be brightly colored, and this green-and-red combo was as eye-catching as anything. As soon as the thought crossed my mind, I quickly ordered the group to put their gas masks on.

"This doesn't look like a poison plant," protested Kai. "Poison plants are usually small. But these flowers are bigger than my head! I think this must be a man-eating plant."

"No way," said Julie. "There isn't so much as an ant around here. If this thing really needed flesh to stay alive, it would have died long ago. Something in the Kunlun wood coffin must be supplying all the nutrients it needs."

"Who cares what it eats?" Kai said. "Tell you what, why don't I just fire my rifle at it a few times and blow it to pieces. That should get rid of any danger. Then we can go and see what this queen looks like."

"Absolutely not!" shouted Professor Chen. "I'd rather turn around and go home now than harm one petal on that corpse bloom."

I rotated the floodlight, shining its beam all around the coffin so everyone could get a good look. Now we saw a dense cloud of words carved into the side of the stone beam. They weren't Chinese. As I looked at the unfamiliar characters, I realized they must be the Guidong language. Several hundred characters of it. This was another earthshaking discovery. In all the ancient city, even in the temple and underground palace, we'd barely come across any writing. Their preferred form of record keeping seemed to be through wall paintings. True, there'd been a few words on the giant jade eyeball, but unfortunately, I'd accidentally smashed it before we got a closer look. Now, out of nowhere, we'd suddenly come upon a whole swathe of words.

Right away, Professor Chen was delegating his students to record what they saw, assigning each of them to a section of the stone beam. Fortunately, the carvings were large enough that they didn't need to get any closer to make them out. As they worked away, Julie got out her camera and started snapping pictures.

Only Kai and I had nothing to do. We wandered around for a bit, looking at stone walls, then finally sat down and waited for the eggheads to finish their work.

I was guessing this would be the end of our little expedition.

The archaeologists had gotten a lot out of this. The murals in that temple tunnel alone would cause a stir across the world that would take years to die down. We had gotten all this other stuff in addition: the giant bottomless hole, the Kunlun god-tree coffin, the ancient corpse bloom. You could spend your whole life researching any one of those and not get to the bottom of their mysteries. Without any protective equipment, there was no way we could open the coffin—even the Gumo prince's tomb had been too precious to barge into, so there was definitely no chance the professor would allow us to take the risk here. Something as big as this would need to be reported to the authorities. They'd deal with it, and we probably wouldn't get so much as a glimpse of the famed Jingjue queen's beautiful face.

It was a shame Hao Aiguo had died back in the valley. I couldn't imagine how overjoyed he would have been if he'd lived a bit longer and gotten to see all this. Feeling sorry for him, I started to blame myself—even though I'd done all I could, there was no way to stop myself from thinking that I could have reacted just a bit faster and saved his life. As my head filled with memories of that moment, I found my heart churning once again. It would take me a long time to get over this.

Kai's voice brought me back to the present. "Tianyi," he gasped, shaking me by the shoulder. "Look at what those guys are up to."

I focused on where he was pointing. It was Chu Jian and Sa Dipeng. They were halfway along the stone beam. Hadn't the professor told us we weren't to touch the coffin? Yet there they were, crawling precariously toward it. I yelped and looked to him for an explanation.

"It's fine," Professor Chen said calmly. "They're not going all the way across. See how the middle part of the inscription is all dusty? The words are completely obscured in places. I told them to clear it away. Don't worry, they have their gas masks on. Nothing will go wrong."

I wanted to call them back and go in their place, but the professor wouldn't let me. "No need for that. These Guidong words are of enormous historical importance, and after all, you're not an expert in this. No offense, but if you were to accidentally damage a single character, we'd be in big trouble. Chu Jian and Sa Dipeng know how to carefully get rid of dust and dirt with a tiny brush. They're trained at this. It won't take them long, just a couple more minutes."

This didn't particularly reassure me. My mind felt uneasy. I was sure something terrible was about to happen. We still didn't know why those British explorers who'd come before us hadn't made off with this tremendously valuable coffin. There had only been one survivor, and he'd completely lost his mind by the time they found him. What happened to the rest of his colleagues? This cave might seem peaceful and safe, but would that all change if we got too close to the queen's coffin? Despite the professor's protests, I hurried over to the beam, ready to summon them back.

I hadn't hesitated long, but the delay was enough. Just as I was opening my mouth to call out to them, Sa Dipeng suddenly bent over, picked up a stray rock, and took two quick steps forward, swinging his arm in a smooth motion to bring the rock crashing down on Chu Jian's head. His friend didn't have a chance. Without a sound, his body crumpled, and he tumbled off the beam into the black emptiness below.

All this happened too quickly for any of us to have stopped it. Before we were even quite sure what we'd just seen, Sa Dipeng ripped the gas mask off his face. He leered at us, his smile twisted and full of unspeakable evil. Then he turned and ran toward the coffin, bringing the murder weapon up to smash into his own forehead. As blood gushed down over his face, his body shook violently, and he collapsed onto the Jingjue queen's tomb. His body twitched, then stopped.

We stood frozen. This bloody scene had taken only a few moments, and now everything had changed. What had gotten into Sa Dipeng? He'd always been the most soft-spoken, book-ish person in the group. For him to abruptly become a blood-thirsty monster, kill his friend, and then commit suicide on the coffin—what on earth could have caused this?

"This is bad," I said. "The only explanation is that he was possessed by a demon. Kai, quick, get out your black donkey hoof. Maybe he's still breathing. I don't think he's dead yet."

Professor Chen was still reeling from what happened—one student lost forever in the black void and the other lying bleeding from the head at the end of the stone beam. Unable to cope with the enormity of the situation, he fainted. Little Ye, also terrified, ran over to lift his head off the ground. She sat there, weeping, unable to do anything else.

The most pressing thing was to save Sa Dipeng, if he could still be saved. Even if there was an evil spirit on the stone column, I knew I had no choice. Stiffening my resolve, I shouted at Kai and Julie to see to the professor, picked up my rifle, clamped on my gas mask, and headed to the rescue. I had my black donkey hoof on me—a charm powerful enough for even the most fearsome demon to think twice about getting too close to me. As for the poisonous flowers, hopefully the mask would keep me safe from them.

Before I could think about it too much, I took a step out onto the stone beam. It was roughly nine feet wide, suspended over absolute nothingness. Looking down left me covered in a cold sweat, so I tried to fix my gaze straight ahead.

I was only halfway across when I heard footsteps behind me. Turning around, I saw Kai and Julie approaching. "What are you doing?" I called out. "Didn't I say stay back and look after Professor Chen?"

"There's some bad juju on this thing," said Kai. "I'm not letting you deal with it alone. Anyway, you can't carry that dude all by yourself. Let's move him together. No point any more of us getting hurt."

We needed to get this done as quickly as possible, so I bit back my arguments and nodded. Sa Dipeng was still bleeding, and if he lost much more blood, there would definitely be no hope for him. I gestured for the other two to follow me, and we sprinted the rest of the way to the end of the beam.

This close to the corpse bloom, it was impossible not to notice its demonic beauty. The flowers and leaves were dazzling, drawing the eye and making it difficult to look elsewhere. I thought of what the professor had said, about this plant containing evil spirits. After what we'd just witnessed, I didn't care how precious or rare this creature was. Screaming "Die, you evil bloom!" I got out my shovel and brought it down again and again, mashing the flowers into paste. Black goo oozed thickly from them. Only when they were completely destroyed did I stop.

Julie had reached out to grab my arm, but I was too quick for her. Seeing that the deed was done, she sighed. "Okay, whatever. You did what you had to do," she said. "Now can we save this guy's life?"

"Yes, quick, let's stop the bleeding." I was already pulling the bandages from my pocket, thinking the best plan would be to stanch the wound as best I could before carrying him back for more first aid.

Kai touched his neck and gulped. "Actually, don't bother. There's no pulse. I guess we didn't get here in time."

I smacked my palm down on the coffin in frustration. "If only he'd hung on a bit longer!"

Unexpectedly, hitting the coffin seemed to send an electric jolt through Sa Dipeng's corpse. He jerked upright into a sitting position. His eyes opened—they were flooded with red. Pointing a shaky finger at the tomb, he stammered, "She—she—she's alive!"

The three of us jumped back in shock.

My hand was already reaching instinctively for the black donkey hoof in my pocket, ready to fling it at him. Before I could move, Sa Dipeng's legs trembled violently, and he fell forward heavily to land on the ground. This time he looked dead for keeps.

Raising my eyes, I saw that the coffin was open a crack. When had this happened? My heart was stuck somewhere in my throat. Kai and Julie didn't seem to know what to do either. We looked helplessly at each other.

If something bad was coming, it was unavoidable now. The Jingjue queen's coffin was open. This surely meant she was coming for us. Kai aimed his rifle at where her corpse would be while I clutched the donkey hoof in one hand and my shovel in the other. At least we'd get to see what was inside that grave.

In that moment, wild thoughts swirled through my head. Who were we about to meet? A beautiful queen or some evil zombie? Whether it was a ghost or an undead being, we were in a tight spot. The stone column was too narrow for us to maneuver much, but did we dare to retreat? I frantically considered every possible angle, trying to come up with plans for every contingency.

The one thing I didn't expect was that nothing would happen. Although the coffin had opened a crack, there was no further movement. Whatever was inside, it had stopped moving. We couldn't go on waiting like this forever. There were only two choices before us: the first was to ignore whatever might be going on with the undead queen, beat a quick retreat, and make a plan once we were safely off this stone beam. The second was to pry the coffin open. Whatever we found inside, we'd eradicate it with my shovel, the black donkey hoof, and Kai's rifle.

As my brain raced through these scenarios, I knew the first option was safer but also unworkable. There was an evil presence on this stone beam. Sa Dipeng's and Chu Jian's mysterious deaths were definite proof of that. Whatever the force might be, it was definitely gearing up to eliminate us as punishment for daring to disturb the eternal rest of the Jingjue queen.

If we were to turn our backs now, it might well attack us

halfway through our retreat, while we were still on the narrow beam. If that happened, there'd be no way to fight back—we'd be doomed. There was no help for it. We'd have to confront the enemy head on and just hope to make it back alive, rather than end up in the bottomless pit that yawned below us.

Glancing across at the other two, I could tell they'd had the same thought. We nodded at each other. It was clear how things were. Even though nothing had actually emerged from the coffin, we were already doing battle with whatever lay inside. Our only option was to take the fight onto the enemy's turf and open the coffin lid.

Kai handed the rifle to Julie and told her to cover him, then spat into his hands and gripped one side of the lid, indicating I should grab the other side.

The thick chains around the coffin prevented us from simply lifting the lid. The only option was to slide it off to one side—and that little open crack showed us which direction.

Tamping down my uneasy feelings, I counted out loud to three; then Kai and I pushed the board together. Apart from the opening, there was no sign from the outside that this Kunlun god-tree had been through any sort of craftsmanship. It looked remarkably like an entire, untouched tree, with even the bark looking fresh and alive. If not for that little crack, we wouldn't have known which bit was the lid.

The wood wasn't as heavy as it looked, and without using too much strength, we'd gotten the cover most of the way off. We were both wearing gas masks, so we couldn't say if any smells were coming from inside. Peering in, we saw a female corpse dressed in jade funereal clothes, lying peacefully in the center of a hollow carved into the trunk. Apart from her body, there was nothing in the coffin, none of the customary grave goods.

This must surely be the Jingjue queen. She wore a black mask that obscured the whole of her face, and every inch of her body was covered by robes, so we couldn't tell if she was well-preserved or decayed.

Finally, we'd come face to face with the queen we'd heard so much about. Though not quite face to face. "What the hell?" I cursed. "You're dead, and you're still putting on airs, hiding your face from us?"

"You tell her!" exclaimed Kai. "Tianyi, do you think her ghost was what killed those two guys? Let's rip off her mask and see if this is the most beautiful woman in the Western Regions or just some hideous demon."

"Fine," I agreed. "I want to take a look too. You pull off the mask, and I'll be ready with the donkey hoof. If I shove it right into her mouth, even if she's a demon, that should hold her in place." Before I finished speaking, I was already holding the hoof in place just above her face.

Kai rolled up his sleeves and reached out a hand. With a rustling noise, he managed to lift the mask off quite easily.

And now we saw her face. The Jingjue queen had a cloud of black hair, finely arched brows, delicate features, and pale, pale skin. Her eyes were tightly shut. Apart from her pallor, she looked exactly like someone we knew.

Before this moment, I'd wondered what this queen might look like—plump or skinny, fair or dark? Would she have a high nose? Sunken eyes? All kinds of faces had popped into my imagination, but I'd never thought she'd look like this.

Kai and I both gasped. The Jingjue queen looked exactly like

Julie Yang. This wasn't a question of a chance resemblance—they had exactly the same face, as if both had been created from a single mold.

My brain suddenly seemed to have turned into porridge. I turned to look at Julie—was she as startled as we were? But there was no one there. She'd been standing behind me just a second ago, but now the stone beam was empty.

Could it be that this corpse wasn't the queen, but Julie herself? I felt goose pimples pop up over my whole body. My mind jittered and prepared to shut down—there was no way to cope with this. Emotions washed over me—sorrow, fear, agitation, helplessness, doubt. Assaulted by all these moods at once, my head emptied out and became a perfect blank. We'd underestimated our opponent. There was no way to deal with this. We were specimens pinned to a table, and whatever happened next was out of our control—we could be dissected or left to suffer, fried alive or slowly boiled. Nothing was up to us anymore. We were in the palm of a giant hand so enormous we couldn't even see what creature it belonged to.

As I was staring helplessly at the spot where Julie should have been, I felt an icy wind, and something sinister rushing toward me. *Come on, then,* I thought, and swung my shovel through the air, feeling it connect hard with something. My vision clouded, and when it cleared, it was Kai standing beside me. I'd whacked off half his head with my shovel, and blood was spurting from the wound, spraying onto the ground. His one remaining eye had no life in it.

I froze. What had I done? How could I have made such a huge a mistake? Had the Jingjue queen broken my spirit? I'd killed my friend, my comrade in arms. My heart crumbled like ashes. This was the end. We'd started out with nine people on this expedition, and now five of them had died in a single day, my closest companion among them, hacked to death by my own hand after more than a decade of friendship.

Now I was alone. What was the point of living? I'd escaped death so many times, but maybe I shouldn't have. If I'd died before this, then Kai would still be alive. Even if I were to kill myself in the next moment, how could I possibly face my friend in the afterlife?

My head throbbed as if it might split apart, and all my thoughts turned gray. My hands and feet were dipped in ice. Only death could solve this. I pulled out my trusty knife, carefully aimed it at my heart, and clenched my teeth.

The instant the blade touched my skin, I heard two sudden gunshots. Rifle bullets clattered against my knife, knocking it to the ground.

A mist rose around me, and I couldn't see anything. Who had fired? Panic washed over me. Something was wrong. Logic didn't exist anymore. Someone was shouting, "Come back, Tianyi! We need to go!"

The voice was a lightning bolt through the darkest night. I didn't understand what had just happened, but instinct told me I'd fallen into a trap. Had the demon gotten to me too?

I bit down hard on my tongue. The pain shook my whole body, and just like that I was in the middle of the stone beam, nowhere near the coffin, which was perfectly untouched. The corpse bloom was intact, though the furled flowers were now splayed wide open, revealing long stamens that swiveled like laser beams to face me.

At the far end of the beam were two people: Kai and Julie,

almost jumping up and down in their agitation. Weren't they dead?

Kai still had the rifle in his hand. "Tianyi, are you mad? Quick, come back!"

No time to wonder what happened. I sprinted toward them, pulling off my gas mask to spit out the blood in my mouth. My head was finally clear, and I felt like myself again.

What had they seen? "My god, you practically gave me a heart attack," Kai blabbered. "Didn't you say you were going to rescue Sa Dipeng? Instead, you reach the center of the bridge; then suddenly you turn and I don't know what's going on. It's like you're sleepwalking. You swing your shovel in midair, stabbing and slashing. We shouted and shouted, but you didn't seem to hear. Then the dagger comes out, and you're about to stab yourself. There wasn't enough time to get to you, so I had to shoot the blade out of your hand. What was that about? Did you suddenly go crazy? Or did the queen take over your body too?"

I looked along that narrow stone beam, piecing together what had just happened. It was clear now—this was the work of not the queen or any demon, but the corpse bloom. The plant tricked people into killing themselves!

The corpse bloom. It wasn't just the scent that intoxicated—we'd all been wearing gas masks—the color must be deadly too. The flower was so bright and translucent, it could dazzle you out of your senses.

No wonder there didn't seem to be any protection around the queen's coffin. This plant was the most lethal guardian. Anyone who got too close would find their minds clouded, tricked by their own memories into committing suicide.

It seemed like we were safe outside the perimeter of the giant hole, but as soon as we stepped onto the stone beam, we were the prey of this mind-bending plant.

That explained what must have happened to everyone who came before us, all those archaeologists and tomb robbers. Just like Sa Dipeng, they must have died by their own hands.

Thank goodness Julie had pulled Kai back, not letting him join me on the beam. The more I thought about it, the angrier I got at the queen. What was her problem? Snatching Kai's rifle, I took careful aim and shot at the corpse bloom, but the bullets simply sank easily into the leaves, not even leaving holes, vanishing altogether. The plant was indestructible.

Sa Dipeng was still slumped over the coffin, his blood now puddling on the ground. He was probably beyond rescue at this point, but we couldn't just abandon his corpse there. Yet how could we ever get to it?

The three of us talked it over, but there were no good solutions. Professor Chen wasn't in any danger, but he still hadn't recovered consciousness. Little Ye was still sobbing her eyes out and obviously wouldn't be any use to us. That was the situation we were in. Nothing but confusion and helplessness.

Then Kai said, "Tianyi, I do have an idea. A way to get rid of that plant."

"It's a pretty powerful plant," I warned him. "What's your bright idea?"

"The plant warps all of our senses, not just smell. Even looking at it is enough for it to take over our minds." I nodded to show I'd already had this thought. He went on, "It can distort reality if we look at it. So what if we don't look at it? Blindfold ourselves, grope our way over to the plant, then pluck it up by the roots?"

"Fine, go ahead," I said. "Cover your eyes and crawl over there. I'll keep watch and shout if you get too close to the edge."

"No way," Julie said, urgently. "Professor Chen's the only one who knows anything about the corpse bloom, and he's out of action. The three of us have no idea what it's capable of. How can we be sure it operates through our senses? These flowers are pure evil, and we can't afford any mistakes. Let's not take the risk."

"So you're saying we should just leave Sa Dipeng there?" grumbled Kai. "Just let him rot while we go merrily home?"

"Even if we leave," I said, "we should do something about that plant. Don't we have lots of explosives on us? So let's snap the beam off and drop it into the pit."

We squabbled away but couldn't agree what was best to do. Then a movement caught my eye. I looked up—it was Sa Dipeng's body, convulsing violently. We quickly stopped our argument and turned our attention to what was happening on the beam.

The floodlight had been turned to its lowest setting, in case it blinded the people on the beam and made them put a foot wrong. Now I turned it up again so we could see better.

Dipeng's corpse was jerking about, as if some invisible force was tugging hard at it, dragging it along the rough stone. Before we could see any more, the light flared and then winked out. A blown fuse, or had the battery run out? Whatever the cause, the entire cave was now pitch-dark.

I banged my fist on the light, but it refused to come back to life. "Spare batteries!" I shouted at where I thought Kai was.

"No spares," came the disconcerting reply through the darkness. "The other batteries are back with the camels. Didn't you tell us to lighten our loads as much as possible before entering the city? I thought that meant I should leave them behind."

A click in the darkness, then a soft blaze of light. Julie had activated a flare. Even this little pool of illumination was better than nothing—a source of comfort in the endless dark. It didn't reach far enough for us to see Sa Dipeng, though.

Now there was a scratching sound from the depths of the stone pit. Not very loud, like the rustle of a small creature crawling along the ground. Or rather, small creatures. Actually, it sounded like there were quite a lot of them.

I shivered, remembering the strange black snakes. "Go get Professor Chen," I called to Kai. Even if we had to carry him on our backs, we had to get out of there. Whatever had crawled out of the hole, I was willing to bet it wouldn't be friendly. It was definitely time for us to leave.

Knowing the flare wouldn't burn for long, we got out our little wolf-eye flashlights. Kai gave the unconscious professor a piggyback ride, while Julie supported Little Ye, who was wobbly on her legs. Making sure we were heading in the right direction, we got moving.

The sounds were coming from all around us now, growing louder and louder. Julie held up her camera and took some shots, the flash sending bright white light bouncing around the space, like tiny bolts of lightning. Sure enough, we were surrounded by snakes, more than I could count, the small-est only a few inches long, the largest almost three feet. They were the same kind as before, with the fleshy black pouches over their heads. The difference was, I realized, all the ones we'd seen up to now hadn't been fully mature. The longest ones here were adults, and their head growths were clearly defined—they were shaped like giant black eyeballs.

These pseudo-eyes seemed particularly sensitive to light. They slithered quickly away from each flash. But there were thousands of them, pouring out of the hole at every moment, piling up and tangling together. The path we'd arrived here by was already a solid mass of scaly flesh. There was no way out.

For now, the camera flashes and our flashlights were able to keep them at bay, but we knew it was only a short-lived respite. Eventually, our batteries would run dry, and after that nothing would be able to save us from their lethal bites.

If only we still had the solid fuel we'd brought with us; unfortunately, the last of it had been used up in the temple. There was nothing we could do now, just retreat step by step.

There were walls of black snakes on all sides of us. My skin crawled to think of how they would soon be swarming over our bodies. Then I heard Kai's voice—"Over there!" He was pointing at one of the walls. "There's a cave! Let's get out of here."

I looked. It wasn't a cave at all, just a crack in the mountain rock, no more than the height of a person. It didn't look par-ticularly deep either, but given the circumstances, we might as well see if we could get inside. At least we'd have breathing space to plan our next move.

First we lifted the professor and Little Ye, neither of whom were able to move, into the narrow space, and then we slid in there ourselves. Once inside, I could see that it actually went back some distance, and there were many other cracks in the ground beneath us—though fortunately, none more than a few inches wide, so there was no worry about falling through.

Julie's calm had always been amazing, and she remained unflustered even now. She quickly studied our surroundings, including the larger cracks behind us, and seemed to come to a decision. "Is it possible to blow up the entrance and keep the snakes from following us in?" she asked.

A few of the creatures had already slithered in and were preparing to launch themselves into the air and attack us. Julie hastily snapped her camera at them a few times, until the flash drove them back.

Remembering how much agony Hao Aiguo had died in, I thought Julie had a point—better to be buried alive than pumped full of venom. I rummaged through my rucksack and found the last of our explosives. No time to calculate how much to use or to work out detonation times, as I usually would. No time for anything but to stick a fuse into the mass and yell at the others to get well back. I set them off and started retreating myself, walking backward and firing my rifle at any snakes that made it up to the entrance. The crack curved several paces on, and I turned the corner to find Julie and the rest safely pressed against the wall.

Quickly, I called out that they should keep their mouths open and cover their ears or the blast might deafen them. Even before I'd finished speaking, a massive boom went off, echoing through the cave. A surge of debris and hot air shot toward us. Even though we'd gotten out of the way of the direct blast, the energy still pushed us back hard, as if someone had punched us all in the chest. My ears felt numb, and a humming sound filled my brain. I couldn't hear anything else.

Kai was screaming something at me, but I couldn't make out the words. Speaking slowly so he could lip-read, I said, "I—think—I—used—too—much. Are—you—all—right?" I had no idea whether any actual sounds came out of my mouth. My eardrums had been battered by the explosion, and even my own voice had become inaudible to me.

CHAPTER SEVENTEEN

THE AIR WAS FILLED WITH SWIRLING DUST, AND THE GROUND WAS covered with shards of black rock. I peeped out from my cover, shining my flashlight toward the entrance we'd crawled through. It was completely blocked—the black snakes wouldn't be able to get through that wall of debris. Of course, that also meant we had no chance of going back the way we'd come.

Kai seemed fine—he'd been scratched on the arm by flying stones but otherwise was unharmed. Professor Chen remained unconscious, and Little Ye had fainted too, unable to stand the shock of the heat and force of the blast.

I placed a finger beneath her nostrils and shuddered. This was bad—she'd stopped breathing. We had to do something quickly. Little Ye had always been frail, and now the blast had taken her out altogether. How could we revive her?

Kai, Julie, and I were the only ones left conscious, and we couldn't communicate with words—at least, not at the moment, the explosion having left us deaf, hopefully temporarily.

I signaled for Julie to give Little Ye mouth-to-mouth, when I noticed a trickle of blood from Julie's nose. I gestured to tell her.

She shrugged and casually mopped up the blood with her sleeve. Then she wrote in blood on her palm, pointing at Little Ye. I shined my flashlight at Julie's hand, on which were the red-brown letters "CPR."

What did that mean? I had no idea what these English symbols stood for. Was she saying Little Ye was beyond hope?

Seeing my baffled look, Julie shook her head and, ignoring the blood streaming from her own nostrils, bent down to start pressing hard against Little Ye's chest, pumping rhythmically.

Now I understood. She'd been asking me to stimulate Little Ye's heart by pressing down on it. Just as I was about to take over, Little Ye gasped and drew a breath, then began coughing without a pause. I quickly grabbed my water bottle and gave her a few sips.

Seeing that Little Ye was all right, Julie stood and tilted her head back, pressing against her ears until her nosebleed stopped.

The situation had barely stabilized, but I didn't have time to think about the predicament we were in before a new threat materialized. This so-called Guidong was in the depths of the Zaklaman Mountains, which it turned out were hollow—like an empty black shell. And we were now somewhere beneath that shell.

This void in the center of the mountain range had put pressure on the structure over the millennia, creating thousands of cracks through the stone. The explosives had sealed the entrance behind us, but they had also jarred the many tiny openings so the sections of stone pressed against one another, then fell like dominoes.

Although I couldn't hear anything, I could see and feel that the entire mountain was vibrating. What had been a small crack above us was rapidly widening, and stones were falling from it like hail. As I watched, the shaking grew more severe, and it seemed set to carry on.

Shielding my head with one hand, I waved for the others to get out of the way. Our only option was to climb upward, away from the blocked entrance. We couldn't move very fast, what with having to carry the professor and Little Ye, and no sooner had we left one area than it became covered in bits of rock. If we'd paused for even a second, we'd have been buried alive.

One foot in front of the other, we proceeded until even I wasn't sure how far we'd climbed. My hands were bleeding from all the sharp rock edges. My breath was ragged, and I could see the others panting too. My heart felt like it was about to burst from my ribs. I was exhausted and thirsty, and my arms were rubbery from the deadweight of Little Ye. Soon, I'd be unable to move my legs at all. Maybe it would be simpler to just give up now, to lie down and let the rocks cover me.

Just as I had the thought, the crack above us abruptly

stopped widening. We took a couple more steps, out of momentum, before slumping down in relief. The way behind us was entirely blocked, but we were safe for now. I reached for my water bottle, gasping, before deciding we should ration our supply.

"Tianyi, are we trapped here?" Kai asked a moment later.

I heard him—so at least I wasn't deaf anymore. Looking at the pitch-black rock around us, I nodded. "I guess so. At least we're still alive, though I'm not sure for how much longer."

Maybe Kai was so tired that his brain wasn't functioning correctly, because now he turned to Julie. "Miss Yang, in that case, I'll say my goodbyes to you. In a short while, Tianyi and I will be off to meet the King of Hades, while you'll be floating to heaven to see your American god. It's a long journey—I hope you stay safe."

"Stop your idiotic babbling," Julie said. "I can't listen to another word."

I was stretching my jaw and feeling my ears pop. Although there was still a bit of an echo, my hearing had more or less returned. We did a quick tally of our equipment. I'd lost a few things while I was running, and Little Ye hadn't been able to grab her stuff, so all in all we didn't have much between us—and just two water bottles for the whole group.

"This will be hard to accept," I said, "but it's the reality. I need to tell you what's happened. We're beneath the Zaklaman Mountain range, and there's no way out in any direction. I don't know if there are any openings above us, but if not, we'll run out of air in about half an hour. The rest of the explosives were lost while we were running, and they're under a few tons of stone now. All of us are either injured or close to death, and the only person in the outside world who knows we're here is Asat Amat—and I don't think we can rely on him for help. He's slippery as an eel, and as soon as he realizes that things aren't going well, he'll sneak away to save himself. In fact, he might already be gone. So if you're waiting to be rescued, I doubt it's going to happen."

"No point in talking about it, then." Kai sighed. "Divide up the water—my throat's on fire."

I set one of the water bottles aside for Little Ye and the professor and passed the other one around.

Julie only managed to take a couple of sips before she choked. "If we all die here, it's my fault," she said, almost sobbing. "I shouldn't have insisted on finding this place. Who cares about the Jingjue Kingdom? I wouldn't have made such a fuss if I'd known. Look at all the trouble we're in, and all the people I've dragged down with—"

"Don't say that," I interrupted. "We have an old saying in Chinese: people die for money, birds die for food. Kai and I came on board willingly. If we hadn't been so desperate to earn forty thousand American dollars from you, we wouldn't be in this situation either. The professor and his students do this for a living. Even if you hadn't turned up to fund this trip, they'd have found some other way to get here. Discovering Jingjue City is every archaeologist's dream."

My own words suddenly reminded me of something: Julie had once talked about a recurring dream she'd had about Guidong. Hadn't she said there were chains around the queen's coffin? So she'd predicted that. And there'd been something about an enormous object squatting on top of the coffin, a shadowy shape she couldn't quite make out. Wasn't that the corpse bloom?

When she'd talked about it before, she'd guessed it was a dream sent by her missing father. Now, though, I found the whole thing peculiar. Could it be that Julie had the power to foretell the future? I decided to ask her about it.

"Absolutely not." Julie shook her head vigorously. "I used to think I heard a voice asking me to come to Guidong in the Zaklaman Mountains. But when I saw the *guidong*—that bottomless ghost-hole—I understood that my father and his team had never actually reached this point or set eyes on the pit. I think they must have died in the desert. As for how I could have described this place I'd never seen, I'm at a loss to explain."

"What kind of story is that?" Kai pondered out loud. "I know! You must have been the Jingjue queen in your previous life, and now you've come back to visit your old stomping grounds—"

Before he could carry on with his fantasy, a series of rumbling noises emanated from within the mountain. It looked like the earlier tremors had only been the first in the series, and we were about to get a second wave. At least we'd had a rest and could keep running if we needed to. No sense just waiting for death. Before we could move, though, a crack opened up in front of us. I swept the beam of my flashlight at the path ahead and thought I saw a figure on the other side. Was there someone else here?

The hail of rocks started up again, tumbling on us like fat raindrops. No time to look any farther. We had to run toward the only open space. Julie led the way, holding her flashlight high. Kai followed with the professor, and I dragged Little Ye behind me. All of us quickly wriggled into the newly opened crack.

Before we could work out where we were, I found myself choking, tears filling my eyes. The air was thick with dust, and after being sealed up for so many years, it was also stale. We quickly pulled on our gas masks. A crash came from behind us. A dozen thick black rock slabs had tumbled down over the entrance, sealing us into this narrow space.

Seeing there was no way out, I turned back to study our surroundings. We were in a stone chamber, no larger than forty feet square, definitely human-made, with straight walls and corners. In the middle of the floor was an ancient stone chest about a foot and a half high and three feet long. Unlike everything else we'd seen in the Jingjue Kingdom, it was made not of black rock, but of a pale gray stone, with an unusual design that was like nothing we'd ever seen, shaped with exquisite craftsmanship. A sequence of images had been carved into the top, but it wasn't clear what purpose they served.

The stone chest took up so much of our attention that we didn't even notice the two people sitting cross-legged to one side. Only when I got a bit closer did I catch them in my flashlight beam. We jumped back in fright, and I dropped my light, which winked out.

"Two dumplings! I saw two dumplings!" I heard Kai shouting in the darkness.

Julie turned on her spare flashlight and shined it at the figures. We relaxed—these were not zombies, but two dried-out corpses.

One of them looked like a child, but it was hard to tell. Both were a dark brown color, and the older one still had wisps of hair where his beard must have been. His torso was wrapped in sheepskin. The smaller corpse sat next to him, as if they were both keeping watch over the stone box.

"You shouldn't throw around words like 'dumplings,'" I said to Kai, sighing in relief. "You nearly scared me to death! These two are more or less fossilized. I bet they've been dead more than a thousand years. We must have stumbled into a burial chamber."

Julie glared at me and snarled, "I knew the two of you were lying. Tianyi, did you think you could fool me? You're obviously both grave robbers."

My heart thudded. What had we said wrong? Did this American girl actually know what the word "dumplings" meant? Surely that was slang only Kai and I understood. Fortunately, Professor Chen and Little Ye were still out of it and weren't able to hear this conversation.

"I thought I told you. I've been researching feng shui and astrology in my spare time," I hurried to explain. "I'm no grave robber. You shouldn't slander people like that. Kai and I have a good reputation. Just ask anyone in our home village! I once was voted student of the month at my school."

Seeing I was going overboard, Kai quickly changed the subject. "Guys, can we focus on the stone box? It's so weird-looking. What do you think is inside?"

Julie ignored him. "Gold hanging off a fixed plate. The ocean calling out. Pull aside the bamboo and see a reverse dipper, a high peak. The moon cannot hide distant clouds."

A regular person wouldn't have made any sense of that,

but I understood exactly what Julie was saying. These were what we call the "lip lingo" of our trade. Because gold hunters have to do certain unsavory things, we've evolved our own secret language—just as bandits refer to kidnapping children as "moving rocks" or to thieves as "little Buddhas." We called tomb robbing "reverse dipping," and there were all kinds of code words associated with that, so that when we encountered a fellow reverse dipper we could speak to them with other people present. I'd met a lot of other feng shui experts through my grandfather, some of whom had chosen to use their powers for personal gain—and so as I grew to know more about that world, I'd naturally picked up their lip lingo. At this point, it sprang onto my tongue faster than my village dialect.

Julie's words, translated into plain Chinese, went something like, "You're a bad person, and your mouth is full of lies. I can tell you're a grave robber—and you're good at it. You can't pull the wool over my eyes."

My mind went blank. I wasn't prepared for this and simply said the first thing that came into my head. "I am no high peak, just a low hill with firewood for boiling water. It is you who are the high peak. Could you show me your pathways and mountain passes?"

"A river has two banks," replied Julie. "Both sides are low hills, with firewood. Vultures fly overhead with no need of pathways."

She had seen through me and gotten me to admit to being a grave robber. Who would have thought this American girl could play me like that? I'd fallen for it, fair and square. But hang on—how did she know this lip lingo? Hardly anyone in China still spoke this secret language, and even Gold Tooth, whose father had been a reverse dipper for decades, only knew a few words and phrases. It was inconceivable to hear such fluency from Julie. I wouldn't have believed it if I hadn't heard it myself. Could it be that she was in the profession too?

Her final words implied that she had picked some of this knowledge up from her family but didn't know the true craft and couldn't read feng shui signs or acupoints. Suddenly, I felt it was a terrible idea to have admitted so much to her, and tried to backtrack.

"I can't believe I still remembered that! I think I had to memorize those lines of poetry in elementary school," I said innocently. "How come you know them too? Do American schools teach that sort of thing?"

Julie snorted. "Forget it. This isn't the time and place. If we all survive and get out of here, you and I are having a serious talk."

A lucky break—for now. I stood up and looked around for an escape, quietly resolving that if we all got out, I'd vanish and stay far away from Julie forever. Or at least I'd just avoid Beijing for the rest of my life—I didn't think she'd track me down to my hometown. But no, that wouldn't work—what about all the money she owed us? Well, it wasn't clear what her plan was. Either she really did have a crush on me, like Kai said, or she was planning to expose us as thieves. But what was in it for her? Maybe she was a reverse dipper too, and she wanted to join forces with us.

While my brain spun in pointless speculation, Kai and Julie had already made several rounds of the tiny room, searching every inch of the floor and walls. There were a number of cracks in the black rock, but they were all too small to offer any kind of escape.

Professor Chen cried out suddenly. He was awake but still unclear in his mind—crying one minute and laughing the next. He didn't recognize us. We didn't have any way of treating him, so there was nothing for it but to keep an eye on him and hope his madness was only temporary.

Having exhausted every other possibility, we turned back to the two desiccated corpses and the stone chest. Even if it were filled with all kinds of jewels, though, it wouldn't do us much good in our present situation.

Kai patted the lid. "I guess this is a little burial chamber, and those two poor devils got shut in here. No grave goods for them, just the sheepskin on their backs. We probably won't find much in here either."

Julie had been studying the engravings on the top of the box. Suddenly, she looked up. "Remember I've talked about Xuanzang's *Great Tang Records of the Western Regions?* That book talked about the Zaklaman Mountains."

"I remember," I said. "And didn't they call it a holy mountain, with the bodies of two sages buried beneath? But you can't think that's these two? This is a shabby little room." I was about to add that I knew about all kinds of ancient tombs, and placing one in a cave beneath a mountain was absolutely against all the principles of feng shui. Mountains contained too much bad energy to be suitable for burials. At the last minute, though, I managed to swallow my words, not wanting to give her any more information that might make her suspect me of tomb robbing.

"No, I don't think that," said Julie. "Though the kid was probably the disciple or son of a sage—and he could probably tell the future. Which means the older guy was his servant."

"How do you know that?" I blurted out. "Is that what it says in those stone carvings? What else do they tell you?"

Julie pointed at the lid. "Look, these images are an ancient prophecy. It's all very simply laid out, and the symbolism is clear. I reckon you can read it for yourself."

"What prophecy?" I persisted. "Does it by any chance mention a secret tunnel out of this place?"

Julie shook her head. "No, and I don't even know if this is accurate. According to the seer, it says that after this child died, no one would ever come into this burial room, until one day, when four people unintentionally open the stone box."

"One, two, three, four, five," Kai counted. "There's five of us." He laughed. "Or do you think Professor Chen doesn't count because he's lost his mind? Forget about that prophecy. It's obviously wrong. For all we know, this whole thing is a giant hoax. You can predict anything you like if it's not due to come true until years after you die."

I stared at the rest of the group, an unsettling thought coming into my mind. "What if this isn't a hoax?" I said softly. "If we believe in the prophecy, then it could mean we're not the group of people it's talking about. But there is one other possibility. It could also mean that one of us isn't human."

CHAPTER EIGHTEEN

"Not human?" Kai looked puzzled. "What do you mean, not human? What would we be if we weren't human?"

"Exactly!" I hastily replied. "We've been together on this expedition for almost a month now, living side by side from morning till night. I think we'd know if someone wasn't human. So what if this little kid could tell the future? He lived in a time of darkness and ignorance. Why trust anything he predicted?"

That was all quickly improvised nonsense. I tried to keep an open mind, and knew we couldn't possibly say whether this child's prophecy was about us or not, or whether it was actually true. If I was right, and one of our group was something other than human, it was crucial to throw them off the scent and not let slip that I was on to them.

I turned to Julie. "Maybe you misunderstood," I suggested. "Or could it be that there were once five figures in the picture, but the carving got eroded over time, and one of them got rubbed away?"

Julie gestured for me to take a closer look. "The entire lid is well-preserved, with no signs of deterioration. There are clearly four people. Look—these symbols represent people—a circle with four limbs and a torso attached, just like our stick figures. Aren't there four of them?"

I looked carefully, and it was just as Julie said. Then she took me through the previous images, each of which was very simply drawn, so even I could see at a glance what was what. In the first one, a small child was pointing up at the sky, while many other people—probably peasants—were running and hiding from something.

The second and third pictures showed a strong wind, represented by a dragon, knocking over buildings and causing devastation. Fortunately, the people who'd gone into hiding managed to survive this calamity. They gathered around the small child, worshiping him—his prophecy was what had saved them.

In the fourth image, the child stood between two grown-ups while an old man knelt before them. These figures were as simply drawn as the others, and the only reason I knew the kneeling man was old was the straggly beard on his chin.

The two adults were larger than normal, and rendered with much more care than the regular folk. Very likely, these were the sages mentioned in the ancient legends. The old man kneeling on the ground was clearly their servant—probably the old man whose corpse was in the room with us.

Julie was right. The owner of this stone box was a child—a child with the ability to see the future. I quickly looked over the rest of the images, and all of them spoke of the mystical abilities of this kid.

By the final picture, I was a bit in awe of the boy myself. This image—of an old man and a child sitting by this box, with four other people standing around—was drawn so crudely that it was impossible to tell if those who stood were old or young, male or female. One of them was reaching out a hand to open the stone lid.

There was no more to the story. What secrets were contained within this stone box? Most importantly, the box showed no sign of ever having been opened; the leather straps that sealed it shut bore no signs of disturbance.

I looked again at my companions. Julie was holding up the professor, while Little Ye had fainted away again. Her chest was rising and falling at a worrying speed, but we couldn't do anything for her. Kai was on the ground, staring helplessly at her and shaking his head.

There were definitely five people here. So if the prophecy related to us, why did it only show four? Trying to act normal, I ran through all the possibilities in my mind. None made any sense.

So maybe the mistake lay in the ancient prophecy. Hoping to find out more, I asked Julie when exactly these sages had lived on earth.

"According to the *Tang Records of the Western Regions*, these men were around in the sixteenth century BC, which would be a good thousand years before the thirty-six kingdoms of the Western Regions came into being."

That was much longer ago than I'd expected. How could we take this seriously? Besides, there were no other prophecies on the lid—every other picture was a record of things that had already happened. Maybe it was just a case of the artist getting confused and drawing one person less in this panel. Then again, even the most powerful seers get things wrong from time to time. I figured we should give the kid a break and not expect him to have known for sure whether four or five of us would break into his grave several millennia after his death.

"What about the words, though?" I asked Julie. "Ignore the pictures and just check the writing. Does it mention what will happen after the box is opened? Any warnings of the danger we'll face?"

Julie shook her head. "No mention. But look, it seems like a no-brainer to me. We're stuck in a room the size of a closet. There's no way out that we can see, and for all we know, the air will run out soon. Why not open the box and see what happens? The seer foretold that we'd make it this far. Maybe he'll also have thought of a way to get us out."

Kai was already in a state of bubbling anxiety. Before I could reply, he jumped to his feet and pushed the two of us aside. "You guys could debate this all day long," he said, "but what's the point? This kid barely comes up to my waist. I don't think he'd be able to prophesy what's for lunch. As for this stone thing—it's just a crappy little box, not even a lock on it. Anyway, we can mess up the prediction. Doesn't the picture show one person reaching out to open this lid? So two of us will do it. Come on, Tianyi, put out your arm. If we push together, the prophecy's not valid."

At almost the same instant, Little Ye suddenly started convulsing violently. Then her legs shot straight out, and she stiffened, no longer moving.

We rushed over to her. We tried her pulse—no sign of life. After her bout of dehydration, followed by the frantic journey here, and everything else she'd been through, it looked like her body had finally given up the struggle. It had already been touch and go whether she'd make it this far.

The three of us looked at each other, not knowing what to say. Julie cradled the dead woman's small body, weeping softly. I let out a long sigh and was about to say something comforting, when a movement caught my eye. Turning, I saw Professor Chen, that terrifying smile still pasted across his face, pulling himself upright with a series of jerky movements. He started weaving crazily around the room. Before we could stop him, he rushed straight at the box, reached out one hand, and shoved open the lid.

This all happened in the space of a few seconds, and we could only gape. The prophecy had been fulfilled. With Little Ye dead, there were indeed only four people here, and one of us had opened the box. It was a shame this kid hadn't left behind more forecasts. The box was more accurate than anything I'd seen before, even after so many thousand years.

Worried about what the delirious professor might do next, Julie grabbed hold of his sleeve and pulled him back to the ground. She settled him down till he was calm again. The two of them had been very close, so seeing him like this was painful for Julie. Her nose twitched, and she burst into tears all over again.

I knew Julie was a strong-minded person, an image that was important to her—she'd never shown any weakness. For her to cry twice in front of Kai and me must mean the pressure had finally gotten to her. I couldn't think of anything to say. It seemed best to leave her in peace for a while.

Followed by Kai, I walked over to the open box. At least now we'd get to see what was inside. The lid swung open in two halves, revealing two tiny stone doors that were sealed with leather straps like the ones that had been on the outside. These inner doors had three pictures carved on them. Examining them closely, I broke into a cold sweat and stared wordlessly.

Kai glanced at the images too but didn't seem to understand. "What's this? Tianyi, you're not scared of a bit of stone, are you?"

I took a deep breath, willing myself to remain calm. "It's another prophecy," I whispered.

"What is it?" he asked urgently. "Does it show us how to get out of this place?"

I shook my head and tried to keep my voice level. "The picture says that of the four people present when the second set of doors is opened, one is an evil spirit."

This is what the three pictures showed: first, there were four figures standing in front of the open box; three of them had no distinguishing features, just like the stick figures in the earlier carvings. But the fourth had an enormous single eye growing out of its skull, and the circle representing its head had snake fangs. It was clearly meant to represent the Jingjue guardian spirit, just like we'd seen on the fourth floor of the black tower. All of a sudden, I was pretty sure this spirit would not be a benevolent one.

The second and third pictures were stacked on top of each other, seeming to show alternative outcomes. In one version, the three human beings and the large-eyed demon opened the inner box together, at which moment the demon attacked, gnawing out the entrails of its three companions.

The final image was of the evil spirit lying prone on the ground, its head separated from its body. The other three opened the second layer of doors, and a path appeared in the chamber, leading them out to the open air.

If the kid hadn't already proved he could foretell the future with terrifying accuracy, I'd have scoffed and dismissed the whole thing. But he had told us what to expect one time now, and it had come true. I didn't think he'd be wrong.

One of us was not human. Which one?

I ruled myself out, thinking I'd know if I were an evil spirit. I considered the others in turn. Kai was standing by my side, and his eyes—the windows to the soul—looked the same as always to me. Always casually indifferent, always full of confidence: *I'm Number One! Go, me!* That was my Kai. So if I eliminated him as well, then it must be one of the remaining two.

I sneaked a peek behind me. Julie was still by the professor, but she was looking directly at me. I didn't dare meet her eyes, so pretended I'd been checking on something else.

"Tianyi, what's inside the box?" Julie called out.

"Nothing," I answered her. "It's empty."

She nodded and didn't ask any more questions. The professor was drinking from her water bottle. His mind was completely gone now; it was certain he'd forgotten everything he'd ever known. With a swipe, he knocked the bottle to the ground, then stamped his feet and laughed like a child. That was the only water we had left. Julie quickly grabbed it and held it upright, but more than half its contents had spilled out.

"What should we do?" Kai whispered in my ear. "To be safe, we could, um, eliminate both of them."

I smacked him. "Don't talk like that. You don't want to regret anything later."

"Whatever." Kai shrugged. "But I'm me and you're you. I'm sure of that. I reckon it's Julie. I've never liked her. . . ."

"Let's think this through before we say anything to them," I insisted. "You know how good that Miss Yang is at arguing."

"Fine," grumbled Kai. "Power comes from the barrel of a gun, and oh, look, I happen to have one here in my hands. You think she can argue her way out of this? Let's just ask her a few questions, and if she can't convince us she's human, well, it's not like we haven't dealt with demons before." He made a little chopping gesture, as if his hand were an ax.

Julie was no fool. Hearing us murmuring urgently, she knew something was up. She walked over. "Hey, what's going on? At a time like this, we don't need secrets between us."

Kai and I jumped to our feet, and he yelled, "Halt! Don't take one step farther!"

Julie froze. "Have you two lost your minds?"

Pulling out my black donkey hoof, I smiled at Julie in a way I hoped was more friendly than threatening. "Don't ask why, but I need you to bite on this, and then the professor too. Just do as I say and you'll be fine. Nothing bad will happen to you."

"Not you too?" snapped Julie. "I know that thing is used to drive away demons. You don't need to use that on me. Get it out of my face."

The fact that she was refusing made me suspicious. I gave Kai a look, and without another word he wrestled Julie to the ground, pulled off his belt, and quickly bound her hands. She was furious, her cheeks flushed. Between clenched teeth, she growled, "Tianyi, you'd better not be planning to kill me just because I realized you're a reverse dipper. The two of you, let me go at once!"

Meanwhile, Professor Chen was watching from the sidelines, laughing joyfully while saliva dribbled from his mouth. It made me sad to look at him—such a fine scholar, reduced to a drooling idiot. It would be impossible to prove he was human. We'd deal with that after I'd sorted Julie out.

"Tell me, are you the Jingjue queen or what?" I asked her sternly.

"What on earth are you talking about? You're insane."

"You look exactly like her," I went on coldly. "Her carbon copy, or her successor. How else could you have told us what we'd find in the ghost-hole? Besides, you're American, and yet you know our secret language. How do you explain that?"

Right from the start, Kai hadn't gotten along with Julie; now his chance had arrived. He pulled out his knife and stuck it into the ground. "Tianyi, let me deal with her. If she knows about reverse dipping, then we don't need to ask any more. Of course a demon would have that kind of knowledge. No point questioning her. Let's just slice her open and let the evil spirit out."

Julie was putting on a brave face, but I could see that her eyes were filled with tears. She wasn't looking at the knife, though, but straight into my eyes. My heart softened, and I reminded myself that she'd saved my life not too many days ago. I'd told her I owed her my existence. So how could I bear to hurt her now?

"Hang on." I grabbed Kai's arm. "We should tell her our suspicions first, before we go any further. If she refuses to cooperate after we've explained, then we can carry on."

"I know she's a pretty girl," said Kai, "but you can't let that affect your judgment. Demons use all kinds of tricks. The way she looks is just one of them."

Julie actually wasn't too pretty at the moment—her face was bright red, and she looked like she was about to pass out from rage. Unable to hold back any longer, she started sobbing. "I can't tell you how I knew what we'd find down in the pit. I dreamed it, that's all. And your lip lingo—I speak that secret language because my grandfather was in your line of work before he left China. He taught it to me. I thought I'd have a chance to tell you all this when we were safely out of here. That's all I have to say to you. Now go ahead and kill me if you still want to. I guess I'm not as good a judge of character as I thought. You seemed like good guys to me."

"Nice words," snorted Kai. "Okay, you *seem* all innocent. That's all very believable. But I'm not sure I buy it. Your call, Tianyi. What next?"

I put the donkey hoof by Julie's mouth. "Take a bite, just one little nibble, and I'll let you go immediately."

"Kill me!" she screamed. "You might as well. I'll never forgive you for this! And when I'm a ghost, I'll come after you for sure."

There was nothing I could do—the donkey hoof was the only proof we had. I took the knife from Kai, all the while hearing a voice in my heart telling me I couldn't do this. Not even if she really was an evil spirit. But if I didn't kill the demon among us, then all of us would die in this room. I still couldn't make my hand move.

Just as this storm of confusion was swirling through my mind, Professor Chen stood up, gurgling with laughter. He danced his crazy dance, tottering toward us. Afraid he'd reach out to open the second set of stone doors, I grabbed hold of him.

"Such pretty flowers," he said, giggling. "All red and green. I found it. I found it. Ha ha . . ."

There was something familiar about his crazy talk of flowers. But what? Was it something I'd seen? I didn't think so. . . . No, it wasn't something I'd seen, it was something I'd heard. The British archaeologist who survived had also lost his mind . . . A jumble of thoughts came together in my head. I had to focus—focus and sort out the threads until they were untangled.

The corpse bloom! Could it be that we were still in its clutches? It was a demonic flower, sprung directly from hell. If we were still under its control, it would explain why we all felt an urge to destroy one another.

CHAPTER NINETEEN

Wʜᴀᴛ ᴡᴀs ʀᴇᴀʟ, ᴀɴᴅ ᴡʜᴀᴛ ᴡᴀs ɴᴏᴛ? Iꜰ ᴛʜɪs sᴛᴏɴᴇ ᴄʜᴀᴍʙᴇʀ ᴀɴᴅ the prophecy it contained were only illusions generated by the corpse bloom, then when had the illusion begun?

My brain ached from trying to disentangle these tricky questions.

Thinking I was distracted, Kai nudged me. "What's up, Tianyi? Your eyes are glazed over. Do we get rid of Julie or what?"

I told Kai to keep an eye on the professor and knelt beside Julie. "You said your grandfather was a reverse dipper before coming to America, but can you prove it? Otherwise why should I believe you?"

"Thief," she spat, glaring at me with hatred. "Believe me or not. That's up to you. But if you want proof, look at the relic hanging around my neck. That ought to convince you."

"Relic?" I reached into her collar and found a chain. Pulling it out, I saw a medallion dangling from it—a gold-hunting charm, made from a pangolin claw.

Pangolin-claw talismans are exceedingly rare. Even among gold hunters, not everyone owns one, or has even set eyes on one. Of course, to the average person, such a charm doesn't look like much. A street sweeper wouldn't bother to pick one up. To generations of tomb raiders, however, it's invaluable—it stands for an entire history, a way of life, and owning one is a testimony of achievement.

Right away, I could tell Julie's was a relic of the later Han dynasty, and the calligraphy of the word "mojin"—gold hunting—that was engraved on it was mighty and virile, full of ancient energy. The sharpest claw of the pangolin had been used to make this, as clear and bright as crystal. Even after all this time, it showed no signs of wear. The whole thing hung from a gold chain and was carved with flying-tiger lines to ward off evil.

By contrast, the charms Gold Tooth had given to Kai and me were much more recent and far less prized.

I spent a long time staring at Julie's charm, reluctant to give it back. It felt so good in my hand.

"It's mine," she hissed. "Kill me if you must, but at least return my property to me."

I let the charm drop back around her neck. "If your grandfather was in this line of work, why do you keep calling us thieves? Your grandfather was a thief too. But listen, that's not why we tied you up." And with that, I told her the truth about the stone box and the second set of doors. "It could all be an illusion from the corpse bloom," I finished. "But I can't let you go until I'm sure."

Julie looked at me, calm now. "Then you'd better think of a way quickly or I'll give you a taste of your own medicine someday."

I paced the room, then came back and stared at the pictures on the stone doors. We couldn't afford to take any chances. If this prophecy was not a hallucination, then we absolutely couldn't open the box without killing one of us, or the demon would manifest itself and slay us all. Whatever I did next, four lives hung in the balance.

Professor Chen was mad, and Julie wasn't entirely clear of suspicion. I took Kai aside and told him everything that had been going through my mind. I knew he wouldn't be much help in this situation, but I needed to share the burden with someone else.

Kai nodded. "Ah, so that's what's going on? You think that flower is still messing with our brains. You should have said something earlier. What's the big deal? I can sort that out for you."

"How? This isn't some game, so stop playing around. One wrong move and we're all dead."

Kai said nothing. He simply slapped me across the face. I froze for a moment, my cheek stinging with pain.

"How was that?" I heard him ask through the haze. "Did it hurt?"

I rubbed my face. "You idiot. You just smacked me; of course it hurt." But I wasn't angry. I knew what he was getting at. If I felt pain, then we probably weren't hallucinating. So this must be real.

When I turned back to see how Julie was doing, I noticed that the stone door seemed different somehow. Rushing over for a closer look, I watched as the carved pictures began to blur, then vanish. It was just a plain stone box now, completely undecorated, sealed with a leather strap, as if to keep some valuable object safe.

I stepped back and looked at the first layer, but that was unchanged: image after image of the seer's prophecies, culminating in the picture of four people opening the first set of doors.

So what was going on? Was this also reality? I dragged Kai over and told him to look at the stone doors. He looked confused. "Isn't it the same three pictures as before?" he asked.

I smacked him on the face. "Look again. Still see them?"

He rubbed his cheek. "Ah! They've . . . they've disappeared. What kind of witchcraft is this?" He reached for the doors.

"Stop!" I yelled, trying to grab his arm. "I just said look, don't—" But it was too late: the inner doors were open. I braced myself, but nothing happened. The four of us were perfectly fine; no demons showed up to slaughter us.

So we were actually in the stone chamber, but part of what we'd seen here was an illusion induced by the corpse bloom. It was far more powerful than I'd guessed, if it could affect us from so far beyond the stone beam.

When I'd rushed out onto the beam to rescue Sa Dipeng, I'd fallen into the flower's trap, until Kai and Julie dragged me back. When I'd turned around to look at it, the buds had opened, spreading their petals wide, facing us directly.

From that moment, the plant's range of influence had drastically widened. After our floodlight was snuffed out, thousands of black snakes appeared. There were five of us then, two unable to move, and yet not one of us was bitten. That had seemed like a miracle at the time. Now it was clear that the snakes had been an illusion.

Why had the corpse bloom made us think we were besieged by snakes? Obviously, to force us into the crack in the rock, then trick us into burying ourselves alive, retreating farther into the fissure, and stumbling upon the burial chamber of the seer.

The corpse bloom was mighty. It captured you not just through your five senses, but through your memory too. Once you'd set eyes on its dazzling colors, you remained bewitched until its range of influence waned. We were clearly still under its power, though it could only manage something simple like placing stone carvings where none were before. And it had made us turn on each other.

This was the terrifying aspect of the demon plant.

If it had had its way, eventually only two of us would have been left alive, then one—until the lone survivor went mad from having killed his own companions. That was the only way to ensure that the Jingjue queen's secrets could be preserved forever. It was pure evil.

While my mind raced with these thoughts, Kai had reached into the inner stone box and pulled out what lay inside: an ancient book bound in sheepskin. By my reckoning, this tome must contain all the rest of the seer's predictions, as well as the remaining secrets of the ghost-hole and the Jingjue Kingdom.

I reached out to open the book, then remembered that Julie was still tied up on the floor and turned to set her free instead. Although it was still unfathomable why she'd dreamed repeatedly of the ghost-hole with such accuracy, I no longer thought she might be an evil spirit incarnate, or the Jingjue queen herself. What had gotten into us? I felt a pang of guilt for how badly we'd just treated her.

Julie was straining against her bonds, tears leaving streaks through the dust that smeared her face. As I came closer, she growled, "Tianyi, untie me right now!"

I told her everything we'd just discovered, gritted my teeth and smacked her across the face, then loosened the leather belt around her hands. "I had no choice," I said apologetically. "That was the only way to break the spell. Slap me back if you like. Slap me a few times." I offered her my cheek, prepared for her to hit me hard after what we'd done to her. If she knocked out a couple of my teeth, it would be no more than I deserved.

As I braced myself, Julie simply wiped the muddy tears off her face, and said in a level voice, "I'm not going to fight with you. We'll settle this score another time, but right now, let's focus on getting out of here."

She reached into her rucksack for a small box containing some tiny pills. She took a deep sniff, then handed Kai and me a pill each and told us to smell them too.

"This is highly concentrated alcohol in solid form, which is why it's so pungent. The scent will go straight from your smell receptors to your frontal lobe, keeping your head clear.

Medically, it's used to reduce cravings. Explorers often bring some of these pills with them in case of exhaustion or hunger. One sniff of this can sharpen your focus, though it's best not to use it too often, or there are side effects. Whether this works against the corpse bloom's hallucinations, I have no idea—but it's worth a shot."

I unwrapped my pill and took a deep sniff. A peculiar, nasty stench rose from it, making me cough for a few seconds. Immediately afterward, though, the heaviness that had been tugging at my brain was gone, and I felt much better.

"This is good," I said. "Why didn't you get these out sooner? If we'd had a few of these on the stone beam, we could have plucked that pesky plant by the roots, and we wouldn't be trapped here, buried alive."

"I didn't realize what was going on till you ran back off the beam," explained Julie. "That's when you told us it was the flowers that made everyone who came near them see and hear things. But right after that, we were attacked by those black snakes, and I didn't stop to think that they might not be real. Besides, I don't think fighting the corpse bloom is as simple as that. It seems to have a direct line into our brains, and I think we were probably still too close to it."

Safe again, at least for the moment, we turned our attention back to the professor. He was weaving happily around the room, completely oblivious. In his madness, he made me think of the British archaeologist who'd gone crazy. Professor Chen hadn't killed anyone, but the swings in emotion he'd experienced had done him in. First the tragedy of Hao Aiguo's death, then the great joy of so many important discoveries in the

Jingjue Kingdom, followed by sadness again as one of his students suddenly committed murder and suicide. All this would be a blow to anyone, let alone an elderly man. No wonder his mind had collapsed under the pressure.

I could only nod solemnly at Julie. "This corpse bloom really is lethal, but we've pulled through."

Julie's face fell. "Hu Tianyi, that's cunning of you, pushing off all your guilt just like that. You know how I trusted you? Not only did you lie to me, you even suspected me of being . . . of being a demon. Didn't you think about my feelings? Being tied up like I was a head of cattle, waiting to be slaughtered—how's that supposed to make me feel?"

I clutched my head. "Argh! Sorry . . . my brain hurts. I need to sit down. Kai, give Miss Yang the seer's book. Maybe she can make sense of it." Hopefully, that would distract her. I sat down next to the professor, trying to be quiet. I didn't think I'd ever win an argument with Julie.

Fortunately, she wasn't an argumentative person. She grabbed the book and began sulkily flipping through the pages.

I felt a sense of dread. She wasn't going to forget this episode easily—I'd have to pay at some point. I'd done some bad things, and lots of people were dead. She probably wasn't going to give us our wages now. I wished my life could be easier, for once.

Julie looked serious, but I couldn't tell whether she was happy or sad. Finally, I couldn't resist. "What does the kid say? Any messages for us?"

Julie continued turning pages. "It's all pictures. Mostly to do with the ghost-hole. Give me a chance to finish."

I sighed. I knew better than to hurry her, so I waited for her to speak again.

Eventually, she said, "You have to start at the very beginning to make any sense of this. The opening talks about how the Western Regions had two holy mountains—the Zaklaman, where we are now. Rivers flowed all around; plants and animals thrived. And there were four villages in the area. . . ."

Kai and I looked at each other, thinking that if she insisted on telling us the story from ancient times, it might take forever. We were both anxious to get out of this tiny room before it became our burial chamber too, but neither of us dared to rush her.

"But the good times didn't last. Some people discovered an impossibly deep hole within the Zaklaman Mountains," Julie went on. "No one could reach the bottom, which made them more curious to find out what lay inside. The four villages shared a priest, and this holy man fashioned a giant eyeball out of jade, hoping to use its magic powers to see whether the bottomless hole was good or evil. After a massive ceremony, he not only failed to discover the secrets of the pit, but brought a great tragedy upon the region. First of all, the priest himself went blind and died shortly after. Then a species of deadly snake appeared in vast numbers—strange black creatures with a growth like a monstrous eye on their heads. Their venom was lethal, and they killed a great many humans and animals. Finally, the villagers sent two holy individuals who'd been touched by divinity to lead their bravest warriors to kill the mother snake, a giant serpent with a human head and four limbs, whose eggs looked like human eyes. Each egg released hundreds of those strange snakes into the world. If she'd continued reproducing at that rate, the results would've been unthinkable."

Kai gasped. "So giant human-headed snakes really did exist in ancient times?" he said, clearly awed. "Thank god those aren't around anymore. I don't know what I'd do if one showed up in front of me."

"There probably really was a holy warrior who led the battle against the snakes," said Julie thoughtfully, "though that doesn't mean all that stuff about a snake with a person's head was true. The ancients always turned historical events into myth."

I gave her the thumbs-up. "Well said. But can you get to the point?"

She glared at me. "After the snakes had been eliminated," she went on, "the sages flung the reptile bodies into the bottomless pit of the Zaklaman Mountains. The gods had told them that this was a pit of disaster, and the jade eyeball had already opened the door to greater calamity. After that, a child was born to one village. This child possessed the power to foretell the future: a seer. Then there's something about the seer's predictions about the Zaklaman, the deaths of the sages, how they were buried among the mountains, and how the seer conducted a ritual and said an important event would happen after thousands of years."

I'd been listening carefully to Julie, and as I understood it, the key to our survival was about to be revealed. My heart beat a little faster.

"Don't look so worried," said Julie. "I flipped ahead earlier.

The final chapter hints at how we can get out of here, but I need to fully understand the earlier sections before I'm sure what it says. Take it easy . . . one step at a time."

Just as she had our full attention, Professor Chen suddenly lurched over, glaring wildly. He pointed at the book in Julie's hands and shrieked, "Don't—don't—don't read the ending!"

CHAPTER TWENTY

THE THREE OF US LOOKED AT EACH OTHER, CONFUSED. PROFESSOR Chen might have lost his mind, but why had he started talking in such an unrecognizably shrill voice?

I grabbed him by his shoulders and shook him hard, hoping that would wake him up. Instead, all he did was shriek louder, waving both arms wildly. "Don't go out! Don't go out!" Then he clutched my arm, pulling hard.

Terrified that he'd do something in his madness to endanger us all, I called Kai over to help, and together we pinned him to the ground.

"Don't hurt him!" Julie cried, rushing over. When she was close enough, the professor's arm shot out without warning and grabbed the ancient book from her hand. Flipping quickly to the back page, he ripped it out and stuffed it into his mouth.

The millennia-old sheepskin parchment was impossible to chew, of course, but that didn't stop Professor Chen, who energetically mashed his teeth into it again and again.

Kai ripped the parchment from the professor's mouth and smoothed it out. It looked undamaged. Just in case he was planning to get up to any more mischief, we tied him up for the time being.

The crumpled sheet was stained with the professor's saliva, but nowhere on the page was there a single word, or any sign that it had ever been written on.

"Oh no," I said to Julie. "The old fool's licked off the prediction!"

"Calm down," she replied. "There was never anything on the last page. The seer's final words were a blank."

I couldn't believe it. Nothing was going right. And despite Julie's request, I couldn't calm myself down. There was something about this room that bothered me.

The seer had proved himself once again. Knowing in advance what the mad professor would do, he'd left the final page of his book blank. It would seem every action we took in this stone chamber was preordained.

Kai and I sat down on either side of the professor, while Julie continued reading. The older man was still struggling, but at least he'd stopped shouting.

"The sage foretold that eight hundred years after his death, when his tribe had long since fled to the east in order to avoid disaster, a new settlement would arise in the Zaklaman Mountains," Julie went on. "One from the desert to the west. They would discover the ghost-hole, which their shaman would proclaim to be the dwelling place of spirits. These newcomers were the founders of the Jingjue Kingdom. When the Jingjue queen arrived, with the ability to see the dark side, she grasped the ritual of summoning monstrous black snakes with the use of the jade eye, and with this witchcraft she subdued a dozen neighboring states. These violent acts enraged the true gods, who handed these mountains and the land around them to demonic forces, while Jingjue City was swallowed by the desert, burying everyone who'd lived here, along with the evil black snakes they had called forth."

Kai, who'd been growing anxious, couldn't contain himself anymore and snapped at Julie to skip the background and read ahead to the part that would help us escape.

"The last section," Julie continued, "is addressed to the four people who would enter the seer's tomb. His words say that four survivors will find their way here after the mountain splits apart, one of whom will be a descendant of the seer's tribe."

"Descendant?" I exclaimed. "Seeing as he doesn't name names, I reckon it's most likely to be you. After all, Kai and I never dreamed about the ghost-hole. Besides, you seem to have inherited some of the seer's powers, having a vision of the place you'd end up before getting there."

"That's right," Kai chimed in. "It could only be you, Miss Yang. I've only just noticed, but your nose is hooked, like an eagle's beak, and your eyes are very slightly blue. At first I thought that was because you'd spent too long in America, but it makes more sense that you have this tribe's blood in you, and you're not fully Chinese."

Afraid that Kai's nonsense would annoy Julie, I quickly said, "This would be a wonderful tribe to descend from. But then your surname wouldn't be Yang, would it?"

Julie seemed unable to absorb any of this. "I don't know," she said, shaking her head. "Everyone in my family history is Chinese. Maybe it's from my mother? My grandfather on her side has an eagle nose, curved even more than mine. Anyway, it doesn't matter which person the seer was referring to. That's not important at the moment. What's most urgent is getting out of here. The next bit of the message says that the seer will point out an escape route for his descendant, but whatever happens, not to let the sheepskin book fall to the ground. If that happens, a sandstorm will be unleashed, swallowing Jingjue City and the Zaklaman Mountains all over again. And this time the spirit mountains will remain buried till the end of time."

"Then you'd better hold on tight to that book!" I cried out. "If the sandstorm happens before we've figured a way out, we'll be buried along with the mountain. What does it say next?"

"That was the last bit," said Julie. "There's nothing after that. The seer must have left a clue somewhere else. Maybe check his body?" As she spoke, she was opening her rucksack to put the book in, where it would hopefully be safe.

Just then, the professor lurched forward, taking me and Kai by surprise. Letting out a peculiar yelp, he shook us off with superhuman strength and lunged at Julie. "Don't think you're ever getting out of here!" he screamed.

The three of us froze, not only because his shrieks had reached earsplitting levels, but because it was now very clear that his voice sounded exactly like Little Ye's.

In the couple of seconds before we could react, the professor reached Julie and knocked the book out of her hands.

There was nothing for it now—our doom was only seconds away. I did the only thing I could, and shot my leg forward, kicking the book into the air like a soccer ball.

Luckily, I managed to send it in Kai's direction, but it was coming at too low an angle for him to reach. So he kicked it too.

The book was now rising in an arc back toward Julie. She stretched out her arms, but the professor leaped in front of her, caught hold of it, and raised it high to drop it onto the ground.

A huge figure sped in front of my eyes. It was Kai, who threw his bulky weight at Professor Chen. With a crash, he tackled the professor.

I sprinted over and grabbed what was now a ticking time bomb from the professor's hands. This sheepskin book, which would decide all our fates, still hadn't touched the ground once.

Julie shoved Kai roughly off the old man. "Are you trying to crush the poor guy? Think about his age. If anything happens to him, I'm holding you responsible." She began massaging his acupuncture points, trying to revive him. Looking at his squashed face, I could see why she was concerned—Kai was very large, after all, for a frail bookworm to take his full weight.

Very carefully, I placed the book in the pouch that hung from my waist, then turned to the other two. "Did you notice that something really strange is going on with the professor? I could swear that a minute ago, he sounded like—"

"That's right," said Kai. "Could it be that Little Ye's spirit entered him? She died horribly. Maybe she's afraid we'll all leave and she'll be stuck here alone."

"Stop talking rubbish," I growled. "We're human, and she's a ghost. If she wants to keep us trapped here for company, that's just selfish."

"Shut up, both of you," Julie said brusquely. "There's no such thing as ghosts. Obviously, the professor's been through too much of a shock and isn't right in his mind. That's why he's behaving oddly. Anyway, if you're so sure it's a spirit, why wouldn't it have entered one of us instead?"

"That shows how much you know," I retorted. "I've got a black donkey hoof on me, and so does Kai. Your ancestral mojin charm is hanging around your neck. Only the professor is completely unprotected, and he was already disoriented, therefore vulnerable to possession. It would have been easy for her to take him. If you don't believe me, why not put this donkey hoof in his mouth? Then we'll know for sure whether or not he's possessed."

Julie swiped my offer away. "And let him get food poisoning from that? No, thank you! Shove it in your own mouth!"

Thinking she probably didn't intend to pay us at this point, I figured we had nothing to lose. The most important thing was to survive. A moment's carelessness could put us in deep danger. I had to use the black donkey hoof to find out what was going on with the professor. His behavior a moment ago had been too bizarre to be explained away as simple confusion.

Ignoring Julie's attempts to block me, I inserted the hoof between Professor Chen's lips and pushed it in. His viciousness of a short while ago had slipped away, and he was back to a more placid madness. When the hoof touched his teeth, he opened them wide and gnawed, grinning away.

"Are you trying to torture him to death?" cried Julie. "Get that thing away from him!" I quickly retrieved the hoof. No reaction from the old man—it looked like I'd been wrong.

And then, in a moment of stillness, we all recovered from the adrenaline-filled few minutes we'd just been through. When we were calm enough to remember the seer's indication that he'd left us clues to get out of this place, we gathered around his desiccated body, determined not to miss a single hint.

CHAPTER TWENTY-ONE

WE SEARCHED FOR A LONG TIME, BUT THERE WAS NO SIGN OF ANY-thing helpful. The seer's remains didn't hold anything remotely like a symbol, a map, an image, even a word. Kai went so far as to run his hands over the corpse's old bones, but there was nothing to be found.

The seer was sitting cross-legged on the ground, one hand resting on the side of the stone box, the other on his knee. We examined his fingers, but they weren't pointing anywhere. Apart from his clothes, which crumbled to powder at the slightest touch, and the sheepskin draped over him, he had nothing.

I turned my attention to the rest of the room, hoping to stumble on some sort of mechanism or tunnel, but the chamber was carved out of the mountain itself and presented only solid rock in every direction. Here and there were tiny cracks, and when I put my hand up to them, I felt a cool breeze. So I figured we must be near the surface, but without tools or explosives, there was no way to break our way through to the outside.

The only visible exit was the narrow crack we'd squeezed through to get here. There'd once been a sort of stone door there. When we came in, we'd been rushing to get out of the way of falling stones and hadn't taken the time to look at the passageway. The gap in the mountain we'd hurried through had merged with the tunnel, but both were now blocked by tons of rubble, so heading back the way we came wasn't a possibility either.

We were spinning in circles, like trapped animals. Then, out of nowhere, the ground began shaking beneath our feet, and we heard a series of cracking noises that kept getting louder. The tremors grew more violent. These were shock waves from the mountain's internal pressure. The earlier explosions had caused numerous fissures to form, compressing the rest of the rock, and now it looked like it was shifting once again. Was this what the seer meant?

After a bone-shattering bout of shaking, the chamber let out a sharp burst of sound and three large cracks opened up, one in the ground and two in the walls, directly opposite each other, on either side of the tomb. They were all exactly the same size, just large enough for a human body to pass through.

"What in the world is happening?" Kai yelped. "That kid's playing games with us. Best out of three? All right, how about we take one each? Then at least one of us will get out of this place."

"No, look!" Julie exclaimed, staring at the seer's body. "He's telling us the way out of here." Her voice was trembling, as if the situation was finally getting to her.

Kai and I turned to look. The crack in the ground had caused the stone box to sink, and the corpse had tilted too. His right hand had flopped forward, and a finger was clearly pointing toward the opening on our left.

We quickly knelt and kowtowed to the seer, thanking him for his protection. Meanwhile, stones were falling from the ceiling, first tiny chips and then larger pieces, and a rumbling filled our ears. The chamber was falling apart.

I yelled at Kai to carry the professor while Julie and I picked up Little Ye's body, and we hurried through the crack to our left. Just a few paces in, a dazzling beam blazed at us, and we looked up to see an opening in the rock: daylight. I could see the blue sky above us.

Freedom was only a few yards away, but the whole mountain was now shaking so hard we kept falling over, especially with so much loose rubble underfoot. We made very slow progress.

Finally, we got to the fissure. Kai knelt down, and Julie clambered onto his shoulders, hoisting the professor to safety. It reminded me of our hallucination in which an escape route suddenly unfolded before the captives.

I gave Kai a boost, but he struggled to get himself out, even with me pushing from below and Julie pulling from above. It took a great deal of effort to get him through the hole.

No sooner had his feet disappeared from view than there was a loud bang from the stone wall at my back. I turned around to see the rock face tumbling away. The entire Zaklaman Mountain was splitting in two; unable to take the strain, the vast dome over the ghost-hole had collapsed. All the rock thundered away, and far below I saw everything fall into that bottomless pit—the stone beam, the queen's coffin, that demonic plant, all those countless valuables, the big-eyed statues. The ghost-hole was filling up with thick black liquid, and all the objects that touched it instantly sank into the darkness. Surrounded by all that black rock, the pitch-dark hole now looked like the mouth of a giant demon, yawning wide to swallow everything around it.

The sheer awesome power of a mountain tearing itself apart left me gaping, one hand tightly gripping the wall, the other holding on to Little Ye. I didn't dare to move. One false step and I'd be plummeting too.

From above, Kai was shouting agitatedly, "Tianyi, get out of there! Forget Little Ye. We don't have time to worry about dead people now."

Kai was right. If I didn't let go of Little Ye, I'd be dragged down with her. I had no choice—I pulled my arm aside and allowed her to fall. As her body tumbled, her arm caught at my pouch and tore it open, and before I knew what was happening, the seer's sheepskin book was taking a dive too, soaring through the dark air.

I watched helplessly as the prophecies sailed away from me. It was a long way to the ground, but the seer had been very clear—the instant contact was made, a sandstorm would blanket the Zaklaman Mountains. Our worst fear was coming true.

It was all up to fate now. I scrabbled for footholds in the wall, hauling myself up as quickly as I could. Suddenly, behind me, there was an anguished sobbing. I could have sworn it was Little Ye. Then my body seemed to grow heavy, as if some tremendous force was tugging at me, trying to pull me down into that awful hole.

My hair stood on end.

I tried to block out the weeping, but the sobs only became clearer, each sob digging right into me. Just when I thought my heart might burst from sorrow, I felt my body weight inexorably increasing, so much so I thought I would have no choice but to let go.

Watching me from above, Julie and Kai noticed that I seemed unsteady, but I was still too far down for them to reach and pull up. They could only look on as the cracks widened and the mountain looked set to collapse in on itself. They had no rope, so Kai unbuckled his belt and lowered it to me.

Hearing them both shout at once was like a bucket of cold water splashing over me. My whole body twitched, and my mind cleared. The sobbing vanished, and I was abruptly free of the force pulling at me. Not a second to spare. I grabbed Kai's belt and rose out of the gap in the rock, into the open air.

The setting sun was already blurry as gusts of wind brought fine sand drifting through the air. An inauspicious shadow was falling over the land. I remembered Asat Amat saying this was a sign that a black sandstorm was on its way. As foretold by the seer, the Zaklaman Mountains were about to be engulfed by the desert.

Kai and I scooped up Professor Chen, who was no more responsive than a puppet.

We had to half drag, half shove him down the slope, moving as quickly as we could. The side of the mountain closest to Jingjue City had already collapsed, sealing the ghost-hole shut forever. We were heading toward the entrance to the Zaklaman valley, thinking we could get through the gap and find Asat Amat. With the sandstorm already starting, it was crucial that we get back to our camels; there was no way we'd ever outrun it on foot.

As soon as our feet landed on solid ground, we heard shouts and frantic hoofbeats from the valley. It was old Asat Amat, his face panicky, screaming as he urged his camels into a gallop.

"You old traitor!" roared Kai. "You promised you'd wait for us!"

Asat Amat clearly hadn't expected to run into us here. Hastily, he pasted a smile on his face. "What a wonderful miracle!" he said, out of breath. "We were destined to meet at this spot! Ah, this was all arranged by Allah."

This wasn't the moment for arguing, so we didn't reply, but unceremoniously dumped Professor Chen onto a camel, then each picked one for ourselves. Asat Amat asked anxiously if the others were far behind.

"Forget it," I said. "They're gone. We'll tell you the story later, but you need to get us out of here right now. Where can we shelter from this storm?"

The sky was black as night. Whirlwinds swooped around us. We were in the eye of the storm, a funnel like the ghost-hole, and as the gusts grew stronger, sand scraped painfully against our faces. Old Asat Amat hadn't imagined the storm would be upon us so rapidly, without warning. There was nowhere to hide here, nothing but Jingjue City and the Zaklaman Mountains in the vastness of the open desert. Still, given that we were in the center of a whirlwind, running in any direction would be safer than staying put. Whether we'd actually get out of this with our lives, well, that was probably in Allah's hands.

Asat Amat let out a long whistle, urged his mount to the front, and led our caravan toward the west.

As we started moving, freakish noises followed us, something between a ghost's shriek and a wolf's howl, but also like ocean waves. The impossibly mighty wind thrashed around us, holding countless grains of sand that filled the air, blocking out any light, bringing visibility down to almost zero. Even with scarves pulled across our mouths, grit found its way into our noses and ears.

After we'd galloped for a long while, the camels began to rebel, and Asat Amat had to let them stop. It was now impossible to hear anything but the wind. He gestured firmly with both arms, and the fearful camels gathered in a circle.

I understood his meaning—if we kept moving, the camels would scatter. Our only option was to create a fort of living flesh and take shelter within the encircled camels. Then there would be nothing left to do but pray to Old Hu for rescue.

I nodded to him to show I understood the plan, and gestured for Julie to wrap Professor Chen in a blanket before bringing him into the circle.

Kai and I got out our shovels, and Asat Amat came over to help after he'd gotten the beasts settled. We raised a makeshift wall around us, then threw blankets over the camels' heads to prevent them from seeing any more and getting spooked. Finally, we grabbed blankets for ourselves and huddled beneath them.

At least we were far enough from the eye that the wind

was much less severe. If we'd remained where we were, the sand would probably have blasted us to smithereens.

Asat Amat's camels had been through enough sandstorms that, once they were still, they no longer panicked. Whenever the sand threatened to bury any part of their bodies, they'd wriggle free and pull themselves upward, always keeping clear of the worst of it.

It wasn't till the following morning that the storm finally petered out. We'd spent the entire night digging to reinforce the sand fort. Exhausted, we dared to stand still and look ahead only after the wind died down. All around us were dunes as high as ocean waves, carved into rippling shapes, a frozen sea.

The ancient city of Jingjue and the black Zaklaman Mountains were gone, and with them the queen's coffin, the demon plant, the seer and his burial chamber, and all the countless secrets held between them. Hao Aiguo, Little Ye, Chu Jian, and Sa Dipeng were buried too. They would lie beneath the yellow sands for all eternity.

Professor Chen poked his head out from the blanket he was wrapped in, smiling blankly at the sky. Julie went over to brush the sand off his scalp. Asat Amat knelt on the ground, thanking Old Hu for his great kindness. And Kai was rummaging through all our bags, searching for water. Finally, he gave up and spread his arms in a sign of defeat, looking hopelessly at me.

I could only shake my head at him. We'd been so busy fleeing for our lives that we'd forgotten all about our water supplies. The point of safety had been passed some seven days ago, and there was no going back. Even the secret Zidu River was now completely buried, and we'd never be able to dig our way down to it. Without a drop of water, we wouldn't last long. I considered searching for water in damp patches of sand, or drinking camel's blood, but neither of those was feasible. Imagining a slow, painful death from thirst, I wondered whether I should have just thrown myself into the ghost-hole after all.

We sat where we were, too gloomy to move, contemplating our next step.

Out of nowhere, I heard Asat Amat shouting, "A messenger from Old Hu!" And sure enough, coming over a dune not far from us was a shimmering white shape. Was this a hallucination brought on by hunger and thirst? I rubbed my eyes and peered.

It was the white camel we'd encountered by the Western Night City, enjoying a leisurely stroll across the desert, slowly heading west.

Asat Amat was jumping up and down, no longer making sense. From his babbling, I made out that the white camel appearing in the Black Desert meant that Old Hu's curse had been lifted. This patch of sand was Allah's once more, and if we followed his messenger, we'd be sure to find water.

I had no idea whether to believe this. The last time we had caught sight of the white camel, he had told us we were guaranteed a safe journey, which hadn't exactly proven true. Still, if he said the curse was lifted, that was the only glimmer of hope we had left.

We got our caravan moving as quickly as we could and followed the white figure in front of us. Beneath the blazing sun, this magnificent creature moved at a steady pace for several hours, neither fast nor slow. Turning the corner after a long, sandy ridge, we saw something gleaming in the sun—a tiny oasis.

Desert buckthorn grew all around the water, which wasn't particularly clear—it looked full of suspended particles. It would be fine for the animals, but it would sicken us.

While the camels rushed over to drink, Julie and I treated the water with disinfecting tablets and then filtered it before adding more purifying chemicals. Only then did we distribute it to the group.

This oasis must have sprung from the Zidu River. With the overnight shifting of the sands, a portion of the river that happened to be closer to the surface had seeped out into the open.

We lit a fire by the oasis and toasted some flatbread. I decided not to tell the others what I'd experienced during that last frantic climb out of the mountain, the strange force I'd felt pulling at my back. It felt like an illusion now, probably a final torment from the demonic plant. It seemed impossible to say what was real or false. Not just during our escape, but during the whole of our time in Jingjue City and by the ghost-hole— there didn't seem to be a meaningful line to be drawn between truth and illusion.

Kai and I tried to talk about everything that had happened since crossing the Zaklaman pass, but it seemed like an unending nightmare. "That weird plant was scarily powerful," Kai said. "Maybe we never actually went into Jingjue City, and the whole thing was one giant hallucination."

Julie, who'd been silent up to now, broke in to say, "No way. Now that we're out of danger, I've been able to look back and think clearly about what happened. The corpse bloom worked in a very particular way—it could make use of memories that already existed within our minds but didn't have the ability to manufacture sights we'd never encountered before. The queen's coffin, the ghost-hole, the burial chamber, the prophecy—all those were things that actually existed in the world. And we'd already seen the black snakes. As for the prophetic images that tried to trick us into turning on each other, it was only because the first layer of the stone box *did* have pictures like that, that the plant was able to create the illusion of the second layer."

"That makes sense," I said. "Great minds truly think alike— that's what I'd been thinking too, but I wasn't certain. If that's your conclusion, then I'm sure we're right. Now that that's settled, we should talk about how to get out of here."

"That's up to Uncle Asat Amat," said Julie. "He's a living map of the desert—if anyone can help us escape, it's him."

Asat Amat puffed up with pride and responded by sketching a map in the sand. It showed roughly where we were, with the Niya ruins to our south—quite far away, with nothing but desert in between. Even if we refilled all our bottles, there was no guarantee we'd make it all the way there. To the east was Kroraina, and beyond that the seemingly infinite Gobi Desert. The north was where we'd come from, headed toward the Western Night City, but this deep into the sandy wastes, it would be hard for us to get back there.

North, south, and east were out, which only left west. If we went in that direction, we'd reach the Tarim—the largest inland river to cross the desert—and if we moved quickly, ten days' journey would bring us to the intersection of the Tarim, Yarkan, and Hotan Rivers. If we could make it there, replenish our water supplies, then head west another six or seven days, we'd be close to Aksu in Xinjiang, where there would be army outposts and oil field workers to help us.

Now that we had water, our most urgent problem was solved. We could probably hold out another ten days, and we still had enough rations left—though truly, in the desert, water trumps food. After all, if things really got bad, we could eat the camels.

It took us a whole day to filter enough water to last us the first leg of our journey, and finally we were ready to set out. We'd definitely be hungry and thirsty along the way, battered by sun and wind, sleeping by day and traveling by night. It would be twelve days before we finally arrived at the Tarim basin. Continuing west another three days, we ran into some oil workers who'd ventured into the desert to hunt yellow sheep.

After being deep in the desert, we had finally found our way back to life. We'd all lost a great deal, but we'd gained a powerful friendship. The bonds forged by sharing such an experience would not be easily broken.

EPILOGUE

I arrived home at one in the morning. After a few days recuperating in Beijing, Kai and I got the late train back to our village. Still exhausted, we waved goodbye to each other and headed our separate ways.

The outside of my house was drenched in pale, silvery moonlight, making it look like something from a dream. In fact, many times while in the desert, I'd dreamed of being home. But I was awake, and this was real—at least, I hoped so. Gently, I bit the inside of my cheek, and the jolt of pain assured me this was no dream. Nor was it one last hallucination from the corpse bloom.

I pushed the front door open as quietly as I could and sneaked inside, hoping not to wake my parents. I'd sent them a message when we returned to civilization, so they knew I was alive. But I foresaw a whole lot of trouble in the future. Hope-fully, I'd be able to get some more sleep first; even though Julie had sprung for swanky hotel rooms for all of us in Beijing, I still felt as weary as when we'd first stumbled back into the city.

Carefully closing the door behind me, I shrugged off my heavy rucksack, only to have it hit a chair that hadn't been there before. My parents must have rearranged the furniture while I was gone. I held my breath, but the night was still again, except for the chirp-ing of insects outside and the wind faintly rustling the trees.

Creeping into the kitchen, I splashed myself with water from the faucet and got a drink from the jug. I shut my eyes as the cool water slid down my throat, then almost jumped out of my skin when something grabbed hold of my elbow.

Where was my weapon? In the other room! I had to—

But the fog cleared, and I saw that it was my mother. She looked worried. "Tianyi—" she said. "I thought I heard—"

We stared at each other for a while. "I'm back, Ma," I told her unnecessarily.

She nodded. "Good. That's good."

"Go back to bed, Ma. We'll talk in the morning."

She smiled a little, touched me on the arm again, and shuf-fled slowly out of the room. When had she gotten old? I leaned back against the counter, thinking how nice it would be to sink into my own bed.

First, though, I refilled my glass. These days, I just couldn't seem to get enough water. I didn't think I'd ever take it for granted again, having learned what it felt like to do without. Tilting my head back, I felt it trickle down my throat, cool and life-giving. The glass was a large one, but I drank and drank, until every drop was gone.

A NOTE ON THE USE
OF OPIUM IN CHINA

Opium was used as a type of medicine in China as far back as the seventh century—there weren't many painkillers back then, and opium, taken orally, was one of the only ways people had to alleviate pain. Today there are painkillers, including some that make use of opiates, which are derived from opium. These drugs, such as codeine and morphine, are legal, but they must be prescribed by a medical professional. Smoking opium became a habit for many when the British began exporting huge quantities of opium grown in India into China in the seventeenth and eighteenth centuries. This turned out to be terrible for China, as opium is addictive and people became dependent on it. Many of them would lie around all day in opium dens instead of working. But the British weren't happy about giving up the income they got from this trade, and when China sought to abolish it, they sent in their gunboats, leading to the opium wars.

As for Tianyi's grandfather's use of opium in this novel, it was certainly a different time and circumstance. Today it is no longer legal to smoke opium in China.

ABOUT THE AUTHOR

Born in Tianjin in 1978, the year China's reforms began, **Tianxia Bachang** (the pen name of Zhang Muye) is a child of the new China. His careers have been many and varied, a winding path of self-discovery that would never have been open to his parents' generation. An avid gamer, his pen name comes from his online avatar, and his stories have been best-sellers within the gaming community. *The City of Sand* is his first book to be translated into English. He continues to write and maintain an active connection to his fans online.

ABOUT THE TRANSLATOR

Jeremy Tiang has translated more than ten books from Chinese, including novels by Zhang Yueran, Wang Jinkang, Yeng Pway Ngon, and Chan Ho-Kei, and has been awarded a PEN/ Heim Grant, an NEA Literary Translation Fellowship, and a Henry Luce Foundation Fellowship. He also writes and translates plays. Jeremy Tiang lives in Brooklyn, New York.

**Don't miss the next heart-pounding adventure
by Tianxia Bachang:**

THE
DRAGON
RIDGE
TOMBS

What should be a simple grab-and-go for gold hunters Tianyi and his best friend, Kai, turns into a nightmare when they are confronted with a labyrinth of tunnels, traps, and deadly creatures, as well as forces from beyond the grave thwarting their every move.

Coming from Delacorte Press

Fall 2018